, ,

The life of St. David

Archbishop of Menebia, chief patron of Wales, and titular patron of Naas church

and parish, in Ireland

, ,

The life of St. David
Archbishop of Menebia, chief patron of Wales, and titular patron of Naas church and parish, in Ireland

ISBN/EAN: 9783741190117

Manufactured in Europe, USA, Canada, Australia, Japa

Cover: Foto ©Andreas Hilbeck / pixelio.de

Manufactured and distributed by brebook publishing software
(www.brebook.com)

The life of St. David

DEDICATION.

TO THE

VERY REV. JAMES HUGHES, P.P. OF NAAS.

VERY REV. AND DEAR SIR,

On bringing to a close the present Life of St.
David, Chief Patron of Wales and Titular of your
Parish Church, it is only just, it should be dedicated to yourself. Owing, in the first instance,
to your suggestion it was begun, and furthermore it should be stated, you have defrayed all the
cost of publication for the present somewhat extended, and—may we hope—popular biography of
a great saint. Nor is this all you have done to
honour his memory. Various architectural and
artistic improvements, connected with Naas Parochial
Church, bear ample witness to a desire, that the past
glories of those days, when David was amongst the
most popularly venerated and beloved ancient
saints in these isles, may be revived; while your

present anxiety to spread among the people committed to your charge a more intimate knowledge of their special Patron, must greatly contribute to increase their devotion for him. The writer ventures to hope, that he has not wholly disappointed your expectations.

The compilation of St. David's biography, in accordance with a plan suggested by you, has not been without its attractions for the writer, more especially as it led him into paths of historic investigation, to which he had been almost an entire stranger. This statement must plead for various mistakes and omissions. Whilst fully sensible of many literary imperfections to be found in the following pages, the writer can honestly say, that he has spared no pains to render this little work in some measure worthy of the subject.

Receive, Very Rev. and dear Sir, assurance of sincere respect and attachment, from your faithful servant and friend,

THE AUTHOR.

PREFACE.

It is usual on the part of every careful writer of biography, and satisfactory to the studious reader, that sources, whence information has been procured or may be sought, should first receive attention and consideration. Such a preliminary array of authorities—very many of which have been consulted and studied—may best occupy those few pages of an introduction. Some manuscript materials here designated were inaccessible to the author; but he may venture to hazard a conjecture, that in the aggregate, these would not supply much additional or original information for the illustration of St. David's biography. To remedy possible defects, however, he has laboured to procure from other available and standard works, or from trustworthy informants, the substance of what has been collected and digested, under the heads of succeeding chapters.

Acts of this saint have been published by the Bollandists at the 1st day of March.* They are preceded by a critical commentary, contained in two

---

* The Bollandists are so called from Father Bolland, a learned Jesuit, who began the publication of that vast, voluminous and comprehensive work, "Acta Sanctorum," first projected by Father Rosweyde, who died in 1629. The earlier folio Tomes did not

distinct sections.   An attempt is there made to illustrate St. David's career, by giving an account concerning those biographies, that already referred to
him. The places, with which he had been connected ;
the persons who were his contemporaries ; with the
period, when he lived, are severally investigated.
Three different Appendices are found postfixed.* The

issue, however, until 1643, when they were published at Antwerp.
At various in·ervals, other volumes appeared, until a suspension
of this invaluable work took place in 1794, owing to inroads of
the French Revolution on Belgium. The new Bollandists—a company of most learned hagiologists supplied as before from the
Jesuit order—resumed this literary labour at Brüxelles, in 1845,
and they have actively prosecuted it since ; so that their extended
Lives of Saints, belonging to all nations, have been written in the
order of months and days, down to the end of October. The
Saints' Lives and Festivals, belonging to the months of November and December, yet require to be compiled and published, before this wonderful task can be completed. For an interesting
and generally accurate account of the Bollandists and their literary
labours, the reader is referred to Duffy's *Irish Catholic Magazine.*
Vol. ii. pp. 29, 63, 92, 122, 151, 213 (Dublin 1848).   The author
of this *Life of St. David* has supplied various additional particulars, regarding the more recent continuators, in two successive
articles, intituled, " The Bollandist Library at Brussels." This
contribution was published in the *Gentleman's Magazine,* for the
months of February and June, 1865.
    * The First Appendix merely contains an account of the Rule,.
which St. David prescribed for his monks. It forms only an extract,
taken from his Acts, as published by Colgan, and it nearly agrees
with the legend, written by John Capgrave. The Second Appendix
gives an account concerning miracles, wrought through the inter-

whole is annotated by a learned editor.* . But this Bollandist commentator states, that whilst many acts of St. David were extant, none of them seemed to have been written by co-eval writers. Hence, it is not surprising, that some things depending solely on popular tradition were fabulous. Other accounts may have been carelessly or falsely inserted by transcribers, and altogether those statements are not quite authentic. Among the most ancient of those Lives, as supposed, was one contained in a MS. Codex, which belonged to the Church of Our Saviour, at Utrecht. This had been formerly brought from Great Britain. It seems to have been abridged from Ricemarc, and had not been quoted even by Ussher, Colgan, or any other writer, to the time when the Bollandists undertook its publication.

A Life of St. David has been written by Ricemarchus, or Ricemarc, called by Ussher son of Sulgen, about A.D. 1090. In Ricemarc's Life of St. David there is no mention whatever of King Arthur. This is said to be a prolix and an affected work, while it formed a foundation for all subsequent biographies. A copy of it was preserved in the

cession of St. David, and occurring after his death. It has been extracted from Harpsfeld's *Historia Anglicana*. The Third Appendix also relates to St. David's miracles. This has been drawn from John Capgrave's *Nova Legenda Angliæ*.

* See, *Acta Sanctorum Martii. Tomus* i. *Martii.* i. *Vita S. Davidis.* pp. 38 to 47.

British Museum.* Giraldus Cambrensis† about A.D.
1200‡ produced another life, as also John of Teignmouth, a contemporary of Giraldus.§ This latter
has been inserted in Capgrave's collection. Leland,
in the reign of Henry VIII., wrote one, and this has
been published in his *Collectanea.*‖ There is likewise an ancient Welsh Life extant in the British

---

* Cotton MSS. Vespasian A. xiv. ff. 60—696, vel. 4to, xii.
cent. In the Harleian MSS. 624 ff. 73—81, paper folio, xvii.
cent. there is a transcript of Ricemarc's Life of St. David, made
in the seventeenth century. It has been falsely ascribed to
Giraldus.

† Archbishop Ussher formerly possessed an ancient MS. Life
of St. David, by Giraldus. This he quotes in his *Britannicarum
Ecclesiarum Antiquitates.* It would seem, from a statement made
by Pitseus, *De Illustribus Angliæ Scriptoribus*, that a MS. Life
of St. David, attributed to Giraldus, had been formerly preserved
in the public Library at Cambridge.'

‡ Published first in Wharton's *Anglia Sacra.* Vol. ii. p. 628.
It was taken from a MS. in the Cotton Library. Vitellius, E.
vii. This MS. has since disappeared. It is supposed to have
perished in a fire, which broke out in the library, in 1731, and
destroyed many valuable papers and MSS. No other copy of the
work is now known to exist.

§ There is a Life of St. David, thus classed, MS. Bodl. Tanner
15. f. 139, vell. fol. dble. cols. xv. cent. This is an abridgment
of MS. Cott. Vespas. A. xiv., with a very few slight insertions,
and two late miracles, added at the end. It is found in Capgrave's "Nova Legenda Angliæ." Also one similar MS. Cott.
Tiber. E. i. 22. ff. 48 b.—51 b. vel. large fol. This latter occurs
in John of Teignmouth's "Sanctilogium."

‖ Vol. iv. p. 107.

Museum ;* and another in the College of Jesus, Oxford.†

Colgan, at the 1st of March, publishes a Life of St. David, which has been copied from a MS., belonging to the monastery of All Saints in Lough-ree, county of Longford.‡ Some writers imagined it might be the same as that mentioned by Ussher, and which had been written by Ricemarchus. But

---

* Cotton MSS. Tiber. D. xxii. ff. 136—182, vell. 8vo. Its subject is the Passion of St. David and St. Margaret.

† Classed, MS. cxix. f. 91.

‡ This learned Franciscan friar, Father John Colgan, published at Louvain, in 1645 and 1647 respectively, two large folio volumes, containing the Acts of our Irish Saints. His Tomes are known as the *Acta Sanctorum Hiberniæ*—comprising only those Saints' Lives, whose feasts occur during the months of January, February, and March—and the *Trias Thaumaturga*, or various Acts of St. Patrick, St. Columba, and St. Brigid. Colgan died on the 15th January, 1658, leaving behind him several MSS., yet unpublished. Hugh Ward, and Patrick Fleming, Franciscans, projected the works, on which Colgan afterwards engaged, but those fathers died before it was possible to perfect their plan of publication. For further particulars, concerning Colgan and his Irish collaborateurs, the studious reader is referred to an elaborate and accurate dissertation, by the celebrated and learned Bollandist, Father Victor De Buck. This account lately appeared, during the months of March and April, 1869, in that erudite Jesuit periodical, *Études Religieuses, Historiques et Littéraires*. Since then it has been separately issued, with the title, *L'Archéologie Irlandaise au couvent de Saint-Antoine de Padoue a Louvain. Par le R. P. V. de Buck, de la Compagnie de Jésus.* Albanel, 15 Rue de Tournon. Paris: 1869. Roy. 8vo.

they are evidently different; for the lengthy passage, quoted by Ussher, is not given in the life published by Colgan. Perhaps, the author of this tract was Augustin Magraidin, a member of All Saints' monastery, and who wrote many Lives of Saints. It had been formerly communicated to the Bollandists by Father Hugh Ward. This differs but little from a Life published by the Bollandists, and which was taken from a MS. of Utrecht. There are other Lives of St. David.* In the opinion of the Bollandists, Colgan's copy had been taken from more ancient Acts of St. David; but while an attempt had been made to polish style, certain false glosses had been inserted. The authors of St. David's old Acts, for the most part, are unknown. Therefore are they often quoted as anonymous writers.†

There seems to be no deficiency of manuscript and printed materials extant, for compiling the Life of St. David, the illustrious Patron of Wales. Thomas Duffus Hardy, Deputy Keeper of the Public Records, enumerates, and partially describes, no fewer than twenty-one distinct copies of biographies or fragments, relating to this saint.‡ Many of these, however, appear to have been composed from some

---

* Concerning which the reader may consult Stillingfleet's *Antiquities*, &c. Chap. v.

† See, Ussher's *Index Chronologicus*. A D. DXXIX. p. 528.

‡ See, *Descriptive Catalogue of Materials relating to the History*

common original. Nevertheless, verbal differences, and even whole sentences abridged or interpolated, may be detected on an examination of those several codices.*

---

of Great Britain and Ireland to the End of the Reign of Henry VII. Vol. i. Part i. pp. 118 to 124.

* In addition to MSS. already mentioned, as serving to illustrate our saint's biography, the following are extant. One described, as MS. Bibl. Pub. Cant. Ff. 1. 27. 28. ff. 618—635 b. vell. xiii. cent. This appears to have been written by Ricemarchus, as stated towards the end. Apparently it is an abbreviation of the Cottonian MS. Vespas. A. xiv. There are enumerated. likewise, MS. Cott. Nero, E. i. ff. 364—368, vell. large fol. xi. cent., and MS. Bodl. 793 (2641.) ff. 221—236. vell. long 8vo. xii. cent. There are MS. Lives of St. David, known as, MS. Bodl. Rawl. B. 505. pp. 217—223, vell. fol. xiv. cent., and MS. Bodl. Rawl. b. 485. f. iii. vell. 4to. xiv. cent. These seem to have been abridged from MS. Cott. Vespas. A. xiv. (No. 356.) A similar copy has been printed by Colgan, for his Life of this Saint. A MS. Reg. 13. C. i. ff. 171—174, paper 4to, xvii. cent. is also known. A fragment of St. David's Life is found in the MS. Harl. 310. f. 166, paper 4to, xvii. cent. It is only a single leaf, beginning and ending abruptly. An excerpt from St. David's Life occurs in MS. Lambeth. 585. f. 61. There is mention, likewise, of MS. Bodley Digby. 112. f. 99—114 b. vell. 4to. xiii. cent. Apparently it is the same as MS. Cott. Vespas. A. xiv. (No. 356.) Also, a MS. Sloane, 4788. f. 84 b. (olim MS. Clarendon, 39.) Paper. fol. xvii. cent. We meet with a MS. C. C. C. Cant. 161, vell. folio. xiii. cent. Likewise a MS. Bodl. 336. (2337) p. 319—322 b. vell. folio, xiv. cent. In addition to these, there is a MS. Bodl. 285. ff. 136. b. vell. fol. dble. cols. xiii. cent. A fragment of St. David's Life, is found, as classed, MS. Bibl. du Roi. 5352. 40. olim. Colbert. vell. xiv. cent. In fine, among

In a collected edition of Giraldus Cambrensis' complete works, published under direction of the Master of the Rolls, and edited by J. S. Brewer, M.A., is to be found his Life of St. David,* reprinted from Wharton's text. It is collated with fragments, quoted by Ussher, and compared with older lives, published by the Bollandists, and by other editors. In a Prœmium to this work, Giraldus declares, that he had been urged by certain canons and religious — notwithstanding his literary engagements, and almost against his own will — to undertake and finish this biography, in a style worthy of the subject. However, notwithstanding such assertion, this Life of St. David by Giraldus may be regarded as little more than an abridgment of Ricemarc's compilation. This latter, as a bishop, ruled over St. David's, and he died about A.D. 1096, or 1099.† Giraldus often retains Ricemarc's very words, inserting a few additions, of no great importance. Any alterations are chiefly confined to softening down ruder and plainer language found in the more ancient Life.‡ The

---

the Lambeth MSS. 12, there is met " Legenda Davidis." The foregoing are all in the Latin language. It is quite possible, many other MS. lives of this saint may still be discovered in various British and Continental libraries.

* See, *Giraldi Cambrensis Opera.* Vol. iii. pp. 378 to 404.

† See, *Annal. Menev. MS. Harl.* 838.

‡ See, Duffus Hardy's *Descriptive Catalogue of Materials* re-

author says, that he supplied some unimportant
omissions and rescinded superfluous comments, in
earlier accounts referring to the holy Menevian
bishop. This life seems to have been undertaken
by Giraldus, from a sense of duty he owed to that
ecclesiastical foundation, from which his dignity and
emoluments were chiefly derived. With expressions
of humility, he declares an intention to exercise some
judgment and discretion, in pruning or selecting
materials for this work, and in treading his way
through a difficult course. His Life of St. David is
divided into Ten Lessons, with a collect at the
close, and a Responsory for the Choir. Such an
arrangement indicates, that it had been composed
for an office or choral service, probably on the feast
day of Menevia's patron saint and founder. This
was in accordance with the usage of early British
and Gallic churches ; when the lives of martyrs,
confessors, and writings of the fathers, formed part
of the daily lessons.* Such custom was a stimulus
to literary exertion. Generally writers of known
ability and piety were engaged, for the purpose of

---

*lating to the History of Great Britain and Ireland to the End of
the Reign of Henry VII.* Vol. i. Part i. p. 122.

* See, Martene *De Antiquis Ecclesiæ Ritibus.* Vol. iii. p. 13.
This practice prevailed generally in the Western Church. St.
Bernard wished that like 'readings should not be taken from
modern and unauthenticated hagiologies ; but rather from such as
gave edification, and were redolent of ecclesiastical propriety. He

re-writing or emending ancient lives or offices of saints. The responsibility of composing or re-editing a saint's or a martyr's life, to be inserted in a church office, usually urged an ecclesiastic to develop for such task his best mental efforts of thought and taste.*

In that invaluable archæological work of Rev. Rice Rees, where ecclesiastical antiquities of the Welsh principality are so admirably treated, there is a very interesting account regarding St. David, even although it be occasionally clouded with the author's peculiar prejudices.† However, in that spirit of Provincial patriotism so honourable to them, the Welsh writers of all denominations have cherished a great respect for their patron saint. They have not failed to investigate, likewise, with considerable research and accuracy, particulars having a special or an indirect bearing on his biography.

---

wished them, likewise, to accord with antiquity and veracity. See, *Epistola ad Monachos Arremarensis*, 312 [al. 398]. *Opera S. Bernardi.*

* " Novelty of style supplied the place of novelty and freshness of facts. And the new reading of an old life proved an era in the literary career of a medieval author, not to be forgotten." See, *J. S. Brewer's Giraldi Cambrensis Opera.* Vol. iii. *Preface*, pp. xlii to xlv.

† See, *An Essay on the Welsh Saints, or the Primitive Christians usually considered to have been the Founders of Churches in Wales. Sect.* x. pp. 191 to 202.

It gives the writer sincere pleasure to acknowledge kind assistance received, especially from the
Very Rev. James Hughes, P.P. of Naas, and the
Very Rev. Prior, Bede Canon Vaughan, D.D., of
the Pro-Cathedral, Hereford, England. Without
such aid, it would have been no easy matter to
supply much of that detailed information inserted,
regarding churches dedicated to the Holy Patron of
Wales, in Great Britain and Ireland.

Dublin : SS. Michael and John,

Feast of St. Columbkille, 1869.

CONTENTS.

CHAPTER V.

CHAPTER VI.

CHAPTER VII.

CHAPTER VIII.

CHAPTER IX.

CHAPTER X.

CHAPTER XI.

CHAPTER XII.

CHAPTER XIII.

CHAPTER XIV.

APPENDIX I.

APPENDIX II.

LIFE OF ST. DAVID.

CHAPTER I.

HUMAN thought can present no more gratifying remembrances, or examples, than those, which exhibit sublime grades of perfection, found in past living subjects. Brought carefully under our consideration, they should awaken our truest Christian sympathies. It is especially delightful and edifying for every well regulated mind, to regard actions and virtues, which really ennoble our natures, when interwoven with the life of every great saint. And yet, it is by no means an easy task, to unveil those acts and merits, which God's holy servants are so careful to conceal from general observation. The hidden life of a saint is the more valuable and instructive, because it forms healthy and vigorous germs of production, whence spiritual flowers and fruit are known to bloom and ripen. But, it is also the most difficult to comprehend and expound. This difficulty is increased, when we are led back to a remote period,

1

with only few sufficient or authentic materials existing, to aid our *efforts for investigation. When
dates are .often conflicting, and when history or tradition appears in particular instances distorted or
contradictory, even respecting public events; we
must regard certain lives of our early saints, in
these Islands, as yet resting, partly in "a dim religious light," like the inner vistas of our grandest
cathedrals, but more generally veiled by shadows,
that have deepened far into remote antiquity. We
should especially desire to have the facts of this
biographical notice sustained by many accessible
proofs or records, and its chief incidents elucidated
from every just and trustworthy point of view.
Although, according to a modern French writer, in
a Catholic sense, the legend may be considered as
the life of a saint,* we are still more fortunate in
finding some facts of St. David's career blended
with public ecclesiastical events of his age. Therefore they become a fairer and more easy subject for
historic investigation.

The birth of St. David was foretold or indicated
to his father.   St. Patrick, who was in Wales
thirty years before it happened, had a like revelation.†   The father of our saint was Potentate over

---

* L. Tachet de Barneval's *Legendary History of Ireland.* *Translated by John Gilmary O'Shea,* p. 7. Boston: 1857, 12mo.

† Ricemarchus, Giraldus Cambrensis, John of Teignmouth, and
John Capgrave, agree in relating this tradition.

a territory, known as Keretica or Ceretica,* when during sleep, he heard the voice of an angel. It admonished him, that while hunting on the following day, he should kill a stag, and with its carcase he would find a fish and hive of bees, near a river; from these he was directed to take a honeycomb, with part of the fish and deer, for transmission to the Monastery † of Manchan,‡ as an offering on be-

---

* See Giraldus' Life, Lect. I. Camden regards this district as conterminous with the present Cardiganshire, in Wales. It appears to have been included within the territory of Demetia. It is supposed, by some writers, to have derived its name from King Ceretus or Caraticus, the paternal grandfather of St. David. The sea lay westward of this territory; to the south, the Maridunenses or people of Caermarthen were separated by the Tivy river; to the north and east, extended the present shires of Brecknock and Montgomery. The Britons called this district Sire Aber-tivi. See Gough's Camden's *Britannia*, vol. ii., p. 524. See also Ussher *De Primordiis Britannicarum Ecclesiarum*, cap. xiv. p. 442.

† "Ad Nautanum Monasterium," according to the Bollandist Utrecht MS. This monastery, we are told, was called "Vetus Rubus," in Latin; and it has been regarded, as identical with "Vetus Menevia." On account of this incident, related in the text, it was anciently called the "Monastery of the Gift;" and because St. David afterwards became an alumnus there, while still later, as Archbishop, he was guardian of those precious treasures deposited at Menevia.

‡ The monastery of Manchan, who was the master of St. Æudeus—venerated at the 21st of March—seems to have been identified with that of Rosnat in Britain. Yet, says the Bollandist editor, it may be doubtful if it were identical with the Rosnat here mentioned, and which on account of many gifts bestowed on it, received for its appellation, *Depositi Monasterium*.

half of his son, not yet born. This presentation would be emblematic of St. David's talents and perfections. For the honeycomb typified that sweetness of heavenly wisdom, which would fill his mind ; while the wax, containing its store of honey, represented a mystic sense, included in historic or literal meaning. The fish prefigured his living by the sea-shore,* and his selected aliment of bread and water solely ; for he avoided every draught that could inebriate. In fine, as the stag is supposed to renew its strength, so the holy David became transformed into a new man, having cast away the yoke of sin, by always desiring to slake his thirst, at fountains of supernal water.

The exact year, when St. David—or as he is called in the Welch language, Dewid†—was born, cannot be ascertained with any great degree of certainty. The Bollandists set it down as happening about the year 445.‡ But this date is founded on a rather arbitrary calculation, drawn from an incident, related in the Life of St. Patrick. It is supposed probable, that this latter saint had predicted St. David's birth, about the year 414 or 415.

---

* Wherefore, we are told, the Britons called St. David " Dewi Deverur," which signifies *David, the Waterman.* Lect. i.

† " Sanctus, quem tinctio baptismi David, vulgus autem Dew clamat," says the Utrecht MS. published by the Bollandists.

‡ They also state that St. David flourished in the fifth and sixth centuries.

At this time, St. Patrick was not a bishop, but he is supposed to have been a priest, and without any definite idea of devoting himself to glean that harvest of souls, which awaited his labours in Ireland. He might have been dissuaded, they say, by some angelic monition, from spending a solitary life amongst the Islands of Hetruria, in the Mediterranean Sea. Afterwards, returning to Gaul, he became a disciple of St. Amator and St. Germanus, until by advice of this latter holy master, he sought Pope Celestine, and received episcopal ordination. In passing through Wales, about the period intimated by the Bollandists, it is supposed, he predicted St. David's birth to take place thirty years subsequently; for they do not think it probable, this prophetic incident can be assigned to A.D. 432, on his returning from Rome, or to about A.D. 459, when he made a third visit to this city, after having established his see of Armagh.*

His father's name was Sanctus,† sometimes called Xantus, one of the Kings of Wales, that of his mother has been variously rendered Nonna,

---

* See, *Acta Sanctorum Martii. Tomus* 1, 1 *Martii, Vita S. Davidis. Commentarius Prœvius.* § 11. n. 10. p. 39.

† Giraldus Cambrensis and John of Teignmouth have so called him. The former says of our saint, "Arthuri vero regis avunculus, fuisse perhibetur."

Nennita, Nonnita, Nemata,* Melaria,† and Melari.‡
She is said to have been the daughter of Bracan or
Brecan, an Irish prince, who died A.D. 450.§ Our
saint was a nephew to St. Canoc of Gallen, in the
King's county,‖ according to this family connexion,
and this latter holy man flourished, it is thought,
towards the close of the fifth century.¶ He was
born in Brecknock, a part of Wales in which his
father settled, and from him its present etymon has
been derived. It would not, indeed, be an easy
task, to determine in a satisfactory manner, the

* Colgan remarks: "rectius forte *Nemnata*, quod Hibernicis
olim feminis fuit familiare, nisi et rectius Nonnita. Sic enim S.
Davidis mater apud Capgravium in ejus vita et apud Vsserum pag.
442 appellatur." See, *Acta Sanctorum Hiberniæ.* 1 *Martii, Vita
S. Davidis*, n. 7, p. 431.

† Drayton's *Poly-Olbion*. Illustrations to the *Fourth Song.*
These *Illustrations* were written by Selden.

‡ Capgrave, in *Vita S. Keinæ* calls her Melari.

§ According to a MS. quoted by Sir R. C. Holt, in his notes to
the *Itinerarium Cambriæ*, Lib. i. cap. 2, and the Martyrology of
Salisbury at the 8th of October.

‖ Colgan has compiled the Acts of this Saint from diff.rent
sources, and he has appended learned explanatory notes, in the
Acta Sanctorum Hiberniæ, at the 11th day of February. See, pp.
311 to 314. This Priory of Gallen, according to Harris' Ware,
was founded by St. Canoc or Mochenoc, about A.D. 492. See,
Antiquities of Ireland, chap. xxxviii. p. 263.

¶ In the *Illustrations* to Drayton's *Poly-Olbion, The Fourth
Song*, reports are said to have prevailed in Wales that he was
"uncle to King Arthur," the most renowned of ancient British
monarchs.

variety of appellations bestowed on the mother of St. David, or to trace their respective affinities, if any such may happen to exist.

It would seem, the revelation made to Ireland's great Apostle occurred subsequent to that previously related. If we credit Roth's MS. Life of our Saint, when venerable Patrick, having obtained his Pontifical dignity, passed through Ceretica,* returning from Rome, he cast his eyes over the beautiful vale, Rosina.† Then, he desired to rest in a spot, suitable for devout prayer and contemplation. Again, the Angel of God was heard to say: "The Lord has not destined this place for you,‡ as a still greater legation and charge await you. The whole land of Ireland, you are appointed to convert; but, this spot will become the inheritance of a boy, named David, who, thirty years hence, shall here be born. Let this prove a sign for you; the wide extent of Irish shore shall be visible from this locality." St. Patrick's eyes were raised from the ground, where he stood, when these heaven-sent sounds had ceased.§ On his range of vision flashed the whole

---

* Or "Demetica intrans rura," as read in the Utrecht MS.

† "Vallis Menevia aliis, prope urbem S. Davidis" (Bollandist editor.)

‡ Yet John of Teignmouth says : "S. Davidem præ ceteris hanc Abbatiam dilexisse, quia B. Patricius, ipsam fundavit" (Lib. ii. cap. 3).

§ Many other things are added in an account left us by Giral-

land of Erin, we are told.* Even then, in the
proud language of an Irish poet, as it

> " rose from the dark swelling flood,
> God bless'd the green island, and saw it was good ;

---

dus. We are told, that St. Patrick raised a dead man, named
Dunaudus, to life, in this place. Ricemarc, in his Life of St.
David, calls him *Cruimther*. It is added, that he remained twelve
years buried, near that shore, and afterwards sailing with St.
Patrick to Ireland, he became a bishop.

* The Bolandists observe, although Ricemarc and Giraldus assert
this whole Island was miraculously seen from that place, whence
St. Patrick proposed embarking for Ireland; yet Ussher says such
account is a fiction, not found in earlier acts of St. David. There
many other matters are seen, which Ussher quotes from Giraldus.
Some of these are reproduced in the Bollandist notes. The words
attributed to John of Teignmouth by Ussher are met with in *Vita
S. Davidis*, by John Capgrave, in his work, *Nova Legenda Angliæ*,
printed at London, A.D. MDXVI. Teignmouth describes the place
whence the whole of Ireland was seen by St. Patrick. See Ussher,
p. 845. " Erat vallis satis magna, in qua est lapis, super quem
stetit ante ostium cujusdam capellæ antiquæ, quam ego oculis vidi
et manibus palpavi." These very words occur in Capgrave's book.
He had been an Augustinian hermit, and died on the 12th of
August, about the year 1474, or 1484. See, M. Le Dr. Hoefer's
*Nouvelle Biographie Générale depuis les Temps les plus Reculés jus-
qu'a nos Jours*, tome viii. p. 575. Paris, 1855, 8vo, et seq. Didot
Freres. John of Teignmouth was at first a Priest, attached to the
Church of Durham. Afterwards he became a Benedictine Monk of St.
Alban's, where he lived about the year 1360. He wrote or compiled a
large volume on the Lives, Actions, and Miracles of English, Welsh,
Scotch, and Irish Saints. See, Joannes Pitseus, *De Illustribus Angliæ Scriptoribus*. Also, *Acta Sanctorum Martii, tomus* i. Martii 1, *Vita S. Davidis, Commentarius Prævius*, § 1, n. 5, pp. 38,
39.

The em'rald of Europe, it sparkled and shone,
In the ring of the world, the most precious stone.
In her sun, in her soil, in her station thrice blest,*

she was still more favoured, when her great Apostle
St. Patrick took " heart of grace," for his destined
missionary enterprise. He soon sailed over the
Irish Channel to conquer on her soil, and to gain
over her sons these happy victories, that planted
Christianity on the ruins of Paganism.†

Thirty years had elapsed, after these heavenly
manifestations, when the King of Ceretica travelled
through a large district of Wales, anciently known
by the name, Demetrica, or as more generally and
diversely written, Demetica, Demetia, Dimeta, or
Demeta.‡ This region appears to have included a

---

* See, that beautiful song of Dr. Drennan, "Erin."

† See, *Colgan's Acta Sanctorum Hiberniæ*, 1 *Martii. Vita S. Davidis.* Cap. i. ii. p. 425.

‡ Camden has given us a description of this ancient territory, which is called West Wales. Pliny supposed it to have been occupied by the Silures; but Ptolemy, better acquainted with Britain, placed a people called Dimetæ or Demetæ here; whilst both Gildas and Ninnius use the name Demetia. The Cambro-British called it Difed, by a change of *f* into *m*, peculiar to their language. Camden maintains the name should be derived from *Deheu Meath*, which he renders *the Plain to the South;* for the Britons are said to have called all this South Wales, *Deheerbarth* or the *South Part.* But, his editor says, it is more probable, the Romans formed this name *Dimetæ*, out of *Dyved.* See, Gough's Camden's *Britannia*, p. 504 and n. (b). *Ibid.*

considerable angular portion of south-western Wales.*
At its extreme western point lies Menevia, now better
known and named, as St. David's episcopal city.
Within this district of Demeta,† the mother of our
saint lived, and she is described as a lady, possess-
ing rare beauty and gracefulness. These qualifica-
tions endeared her to the king.‡ From the time of
St. David's conception,§ we are told, that she lived
solely on bread and water, afterwards leading a celi-
bate's life. While yet in his mother's womb, the

---

* As laid down in the *Atlas Classica*, Demeta seems to com-
prise the Shires of Pembroke, Cardigan, and Caermarthen. See,
the edition of this work, published by Robert Wilkinson, London,
1808. Royal 4to.

† The Demetian or Demetican territory—the site of which has
been placed by Ptolemy in Britain—is said to have contained Pembroke, Caermarthen, and Ceretica districts. But this supposition
appears contrary to what is related in St. David's Acts, viz., that
his father set out from Ceretica and went into Demetica. " *Menevia,
sila est in Penbrokiæ Commitatus promontorio spacioso, quod grandi
fronte in Oceanum Verginium longe procedit:* ὀκταπίταρον ἄκρον
appellat Ptolemæus, Britanni incolæ Pebidiauc & Cantred-Dewi,
Angli S. David's-land, *id est* S. Davidis ditionem, & *ipsam urbem*
Meneviam *Britanni* Tuy-Deui, *id est* domus Deui *sive* Davidis, *et
Angli* S. Dauida *appellant.*" See, *Acta Sanctorum Martii, tomus*
i., *Martii* i. *Vita S. Davidis, Commentarius Prævius.* § i, n. 4, p.
38.

‡ We are told, he met Nonnita, when " ad partes de Pepidiauc
declinaverat." *Lect.* i.

§ Referring to this incident, the Utrecht MS. relates a legend
not found in Roth's MS.

advent of our saint was signalized by miracles.
Shortly before his birth, the mother entered a certain church,* where a very celebrated and holy man,
named Gildas,† preached God's word to the people.
As if struck suddenly dumb, on her entering, the
preacher ceased his discourse; and declared, on
being asked the reason for this silence, he felt unable to announce divine truths in the ordinary way.
He then requested his congregation to leave the
church ; and no other persons remained within, but
our saint's mother, who continued there unknown to
the preacher. Yet, another attempt to speak made
by this holy teacher was not attended with better
success. Wherefore, raising his voice, he adjured
any person yet remaining to reveal the fact. Our
saint's mother then made known her presence. The
preacher requested her to leave the church, so that
his congregation might return. This order having
been obeyed, the holy man found his tongue, capable
of giving expression to his ordinary religious and
impressive sermons. Thus did the Almighty mani-

---

* " Ad offerendas pro partu eleemosynas oblationem," says the
Utrecht MS. Alluding to the site of this church Giraldus Cambrensis writes, that it was situated in a place called Kanmorva or
Cair Morua, which means *a Maritime Fort* or *town*, in the English language. See, *Vita S. Davidis.* John Capgrave has a similar account, in his Life of our Saint.

† Known as, St. Gildas the Wise. His feast is kept on the 29th
of January.

fest his power, and indicate to all present, the future
greatness and eloquence of an unborn child.* Like
the Blessed Virgin Mary, we can have little doubt,
his mother treasured these remarkable incidents
within her heart.†

When the Saviour of this world deigned to en-
lighten it by his presence, the wicked tyrant Herod
sought to learn the place of his birth, from those
pilgrim Magi, that came from the East to adore him.
This monster, however, designed the infant Saviour's
death.‡ As happened in the case of our Divine
Master, a tyrant of Demeta planned the infanticide
of David, when his birth had occurred. This wicked
and envious man had learned from British Magi,
the whole country around must become subject to
that child, after his being born. They had even
pointed out the exact place, where his mother would
be found living, when her term of child-bearing had
elapsed. The Almighty, however, miraculously preserved the pious matron and her infant charge.§

---

* See, *Colgan's Acta Sanctorum Hiberniæ*, 1 *Martii, Vita S.
Davidis.* Cap. iii. iv. pp. 425, 426.

† See *Luke*, ii. 19.

‡ *Matthew*, ii.

§ The Utrecht MS. contains the following legend, not to be
found in Roth's MS., and referring to the time of St. David's birth:
" Urgente vero dolore in petra, quæ juxta erat, manibus innixa est :
quæ vestigium veluti cera impressum, petram intuentibus ostendit :
quæ et in medium divisa dole iti matri condoluit." And Capgrave

At the very moment of St. David's birth, a mighty tempest, mingled with lightning, hail, thunder and rain, swept the whole country around, so that no person dare venture out of doors. Yet, by a strange contrast, the air was perfectly serene, the skies were lightsome, nor did any storms prevail; near the house, where this religious woman experienced the pains and consolations of such heaven-protected maternity.* In this physical world, storms and aerial disturbances are required to render our atmosphere clear and salubrious : the moral order of our lives is usually purified by chastening persecutions and afflictions.

If he were a grandson to the Irish prince, Bracan, or Brecan, by his mother's side, and a nephew to St. Canoc of Gallen, he could hardly have been born in the year 462.† Some writers maintain his birth

---

tells us, that a church was afterwards built on this spot, while the stone itself rested as a foundation for its altar, which covered the stone.—*Legenda Sanctorum Angliæ.*

* See, *Colgan's Acta Sanctorum Hiberniæ.* 1 *Martii. Vita S. Davidis.* Cap. v. p. 426.

† In the Acts of St. David, it is said, when St. Patrick happened to be in the *Vallis Rosina,* in which Menevia was situated, an Angel foretold, that after thirty years a child would be born. He should bear the name of David, it was announced, and at a proper time, he would have care of that place. Soon afterwards St. Patrick set out for Ireland, where he arrived in the year 432. Hence Ussher has concluded, that St. David was born in 462. See *Britannicarum Ecclesiarum Antiquitates,* cap. xvii. p. 452; and *Index Chronologicus,* A.D. CCCCLXII. p. 521.

occurred at this date, upon an unproved supposition, that he came into the world, thirty years after St. Patrick was about to arrive in Ireland, when engaging on his great mission.* Now we are also informed, that soon after his birth, St. David was baptized by St. Helvacus, otherwise, Ailbe, the Bishop of Munster. Hardly can we believe that St. Ailbe was bishop so early as 462; yet this is not very clear. We have a further probable indication regarding David not having been born at this date, from what we find mentioned, concerning his birth and future greatness having been predicted by this Ailbe.†

---

* Ussher's calculation would answer very well, if it could be proved the Angel spoke in that manner. For as to the opinion of writers of our Saint's Acts, viz., that David was born in 462, if they thought so, their authority is still of little weight. We do not know, whether they were rightly informed concerning the year of St. Patrick's arrival in Ireland. The notation of thirty intermediate years cannot then form a correct chronological date. "I do not know," writes Dr. Lanigan, "how it came to pass that the compilers of the Acts of our saints were so fond of the number *thirty,* as we have seen in the accounts of St. Patrick, St. Brigid, St. Finnian, &c. Jocelin gives a different turn to that prophecy, and attributing one somewhat like it to St. Patrick himself, who, he says (cap. 167), happening to be in Britain some years after the commencement of his mission, foretold the sanctity of St. David then in his mother's womb." See *Ecclesiastical History of Ireland,* vol. i. chap. ix. § ix. n. 136, pp. 471, 472.

† Ailbe's reputation until about A.D. 490, had not been so generally established, as to have had predictions of this sort attributed to

Immediately at his birth, he was baptized, according to one account, by Bishop Elisus ;* but, other
writers call him Helveus or Ailbeus, Bishop of
Munster.† St. David gave sight to a blind man,

---

him. If then, we may be allowed to build upon such traditions,
David's birth must be brought down to the close of the fifth century
or perhaps to the beginning of the sixth. Meanwhile, those thirty
years, already treated of, must be omitted from such calculations.
See, *Ibid.* n. 138., p. 472.

* This is stated, not only in St. David's Life, but also in the Acts
of St. Ailbe, which Colgan promised to give at the 12th of September, his feast day. But we are admonished, that this baptism
by Ailbeus did not take place before A.D. 432, when St. Patrick
journeyed from Italy through Britain, on his way to Ireland. It
took place on a subsequent occasion, A.D. 462, according to Colgan, when St. Ailbe is thought to have been in this part of Wales.
See, *Acta Sanctorum Hiberniæ*, i. *Martii, Vita S. Davidis*, n. 8, p.
431.

† Giraldus writes, that St. David was born at a place near the
present St. David's, and that he was baptised at Porth Clais or
Portcleis, by Ælueus, or Albeus, Bishop of Munster. Ussher
says, that Portcleis was near Menevia, and that its name had not
been changed even in his time. Giraldus Cambrensis, in his Life
of St. David, according to the old edition, instead of Ailbe, has
Relveus, Bishop of *Menevia*, who, he says, had just arrived in
Britain, from Ireland. But, as Ussher observes (p. 871), there
was no Bishop of Menevia before St. David, and as Giraldus himself allows, he first built there a cathedral church. No necessity
for this observation exists, if we follow Wharton's edition in *Anglia
Sacra*, tom. ii. Giraldus' text here is *Aelveo Muveniensium episcopi*, and it plainly refers to Ailbe, Bishop of Munster. In the life
of this latter holy man, David's father is said to have given his son

who held him, whilst the water was being poured
upon him.　We are again told, this blind man used
as a lotion for his eyes, that very water, which had
flowed on the head of David, during his baptism.
This act the infant is supposed to have performed
through some holy inspiration.　In the very same
place, a beautiful and clear fountain of water sprung
from earth.　It served for the matter of baptism.
As the rising sun dispels the shades of night, so
this newly born child gave sight to the blind, and
he enlightened, likewise, in a miraculous manner,
the pagan society of his age and country.

---

to St. Albeus, "ut nutriret eum Deo."　And afterwards it is stated:　·
" Ipse est David sanctus Episcopus : cujus reliquiæ requiescunt in
civitate sua Ceallmuni, quæ est in Britannia."

CHAPTER II.

The Monastery of Rosnat or Kilmune.—St. David nurtured in Old
Menevia.—The Dove, an emblem of his innocence and holiness.—It is probable, St. David and St. Finnian of Clonard
were early companions.

FROM allusions already made to this celebrated
Monastery of Manchen, it is somewhat incumbent
on us to trace out—so far as can possibly be done—
both its origin and that of its founder. Yet, it will
not be an easy matter to determine, who was this
Manchan, or as he is sometimes called, Nennius,
under various forms of writing. There are divers
reasons adduced, for supposing him to have been an
Irishman, by race and birth. In any history or
Martyrology known, we cannot find one bearing
such a name, and belonging to the British nation.*
Yet, we must endeavour to discover one having this
cognomen, who had attained some degree of celebrity, even before St. David's birth, and who settled
in the valley of Rosnat, where he lived in a Monastery, known as Kill-mune. Such attempt would

---

* There may have been an exception, in the particular case of
Nennius of Bangor—if he were a Briton by birth—but he is said
by Camerarius, to have first become a monk, about the year 600,
and as other writers state, he flourished, *circiter*, 620. See,
Bale, *Britannicarum Rerum Scriptores*, n. 67.

2

lead us to a conclusion, that Manchan probably lived before, or at least soon after the commencement of the fifth century. In our Irish calendars, as we are told, are found many different saints bearing this name, and their Natales occur as follows,* viz.: At January, 2nd,† 13th,‡ and 24th;§ at February 14th;|| at March 1st;¶ at May 21st;** at October 12th;†† at November 2nd;‡‡ and at Decem-

---

* They are enumerated, as found in the text, by St. Ængus, by the Martyrology of Tallagh, by Marianus Gorman, by Maguire, and by the Martyrology of Donegall.

† At this day, Mainchin, the Sage of Disert-mic-Cuillin of Laeighis in Leinster, is venerated. See, *The Martyrology of Donegall*, edited by Drs. Todd and Reeves, pp. 4, 5.

‡ At this day was venerated Mainchin, son of Collan, in Corann. *Ibid.*, pp. 14, 15.

§ On this day, we find the feast of Manchan, of Liath, son of Indagh.—*Ibid.* pp. 26, 27.

|| Mainchein of Moethail is venerated on this day.—*Ibid.* pp. 48, 49.

¶ At this day, I can only discover a Maoineann, bishop of Cluain-ferta-Brenainn, as nearly approaching the name Manchan. See, *Ibid.* pp. 60, 61. In the Rev. Dr. Kelly's *Martyrology of Tallagh*, he is set down as "Moinend, Epis." at the same day. See, p. xvii.

** At this day, I only find a "Moinne;" in *The Martyrology of Donegall*, pp. 134, 135. In the *Martyrology of Tallagh*, he is thus entered, "Moenind ocus Polan." See, p. xxv.

†† Neither in the *Martyrology of Tallagh*, or in the *Martyrology of Donegall*, do I find a St. Manchan, so called. In the latter, however, we have recorded a Nannidh of Inis Cais. See, pp. 274, 275.

‡‡ At this date, Dr. Kelly's *Martyrology of Tallagh* fails, but

ber 4th.* Again, if we regard the denomination,
Nennius, Nennidius, or Nennionus, we find Irish
saints, not fewer in number, set down in our calen-
dars. Among these, we need only mention, St.
Nennius, abbot of Inis-muighe-Samh, on Lough
Erne, at the 16th and 18th of January;† St.
Moinennus or Mon-Nennius at the 1st of March;‡
St. Nennionus or Nennius, denominated Sene of the
Monastery, at the 18th of April;§ St. Nennius,
abbot of Clon-chaoin, at the 21st of April;‖ St.
Nennius, Deacon of Cluain-airthir, at the 25th of

---

even in *The Martyrology of Donegall*, I cannot find notice of a
Manchan, at this day.

* The previous remarks apply to this particular date.

† Colgan gives us his Acts, at the latter of these days. It is
said, he flourished in the time of Saints Patrick and Brigid; that
he left Ireland; and that he lived many years afterwards in
Britain.

‡ Colgan published his Acts, at this day. He is there called
Bishop of Clonfert. He flourished, about the middle of the sixth
century. See, *Acta Sanctorum Hiberniæ*, 1 *Martii*. *Vita S.
Moinenni, sive, Mon-Nennii*, pp. 437 to 439.

§ In *The Martyrology of Donegall*, already quoted, I find nothing regarding him. But, in the *Martyrology of Tallagh*, I meet
with a " Moninnsen o Mainister," at this date, p. xxi.

‖ There is a Ninnidh of Cluain-Caoi, at this day in *The Martyrology of Donegall*, pages 106, 107. Dr. Kelly's *Martyrology
of Tallagh* does not mention him at this date, in such a
manner; but we find there a " Ninidh Bugno i Tir Bret." See,
page xxii.

April ;* St. Nennius Sene, at the 25th of July;†
St. Nennius, Bishop of Kiltoma, in Meath, at the
13th of November.‡ Colgan is of opinion, that the
founder of Kill-mune—sometimes called Nennius—
can be no other person, than the saint having this
name, venerated on the 1st of March, and who had
so many Irish saints enumerated among his disciples, viz. : Saints Brigid, Virgin,§ Endeus,‖
Finnian of Maghbile,¶ Tigernach,** Eugene, Bishop

---

* In *The Martyrology of Donegall*, there is a notice concerning
Deacon Menn of Cluain Arathair, at this date. In a note, he
seems to be identical with Nennius, as the commentator remarks.
See, pp. 110, 111. In the *Martyrology of Tallagh*, we read,
" Dechonen Cluana Arathair." See, p. xxii.

† In *The Martyrology of Donegall*, at this date, he is called,
Ninnio, the old. In the *Martyrology of Tallagh*, he is denominated, " Ninnio senior." See, p. xxx.

‡ In *The Martyrology of Donegall*, at this date, such an entry
may be seen, pp. 308, 309. Dr. Kelly's *Martyrology of Tallagh*
fails at this month.

§ So Colgan states. But, I fear he must have hastily identified
this saint, with *Ninnidh of the White Hand*, whose acts he gives
at the 18th of January.

‖ In the life of this saint, published by Colgan, at the 21st of
March, his sister St. Fanchea is represented as saying to him :
" Vade ad Britanniam ad Rosnacum monasterium, et esto humilis
discipulus Manseni, Magistri illius Monasterii." See, cap. v. p. 705.

¶ " Ut habetur in ejus vita, cap. iii.," says Colgan.

** This saint, who is venerated on the 4th of April, was dili-
gently instructed, " Monennii disciplinis et monitis in Rosnacensi
Monasterio, quod alio nomine Alba vocatur." *Vita S. Tigernaci*,
cap. iii.

of Ardstra,* and Carpre, Bishop of Colerain.†
Whoever had been master of these great saints,
must necessarily have flourished, before the end of
the fifth century.

From what we have already said, there seems to
be little difficulty in reconciling the chronological
period of the exiled Irish Manchan, living in Wales,
with that of a holy man, known as Manchen the
Máster.‡ He is classed among the disciples of St.
Patrick, our great Irish Apostle. It is said, this
latter had set him to rule over the church of Coille
Fochluc, in Connaught.§ All upon record might
agree with the holy character, wisdom, and learning
of the saintly abbot Manchan, who presided over
Rosnat or Kill-mune Monastery, in Britain, and perhaps, at some subsequent period of his life.

When Manchan and probably some Irish disciples

---

* As in the former instance, we find Rosnacensis or Rosnatensis,
confounded with Alba, and Nennius or Monennius with Mancha-
nus, so in *Vita S. Eugenii*, cap. iii., as Colgan promised to show
at the 23rd of August, these words are quoted, " Vir sanctus ac
sapiens, Nennio qui Mancenus dicitur de Rosnacensi Monasterio
quod alio nomine Alba vocatur."

† Also, *Vita S. Eugenii*, cap. iii., quoted by Colgan.

‡ See, *Vita Tripartita S. Patricii, Pars.* ii. cap. 62. Colgan's
Trias Thaumaturga.

§ So says Joceline. " Sanctus etiam Patricius huic populo con-
verso noviter ad Christum, Magistrum, Manchenum virum re-
ligeosum, et in scripturis sanctis exercitatum. *Vita S. Patricii,*
cap. 59. *Ibid.*

alone were inhabitants of this place, they may have
given it the well-remembered name Kill-mune. By
this denomination, it seems to have been solely
designated in all our Irish Histories and Calendars.
Possibly, it obtained the title, *Monasterium Rosna-
tense* or *Rosnacense*, in other writings, from the
circumstance of Manchan's religious house having
been built in the valley Rosina or Rosnat. We know,
that Menevia or St. David's afterwards lay in this
valley.* It does not seem so clearly explained why
this place had the etymon, *Alba*, applied to it.†
Yet Colgan was doubtful if this monastery, called
indiscriminately in the lives of our early saints, Ros-
natense, Albium or Magnum Monasterium, could
have been different from that of Benchor or Bangor.‡
Such a supposition, however, would even appear
irreconcilable with various authorities produced by
this learned author.

---

* See, Giraldus Cambrensis, *Itinerarium Cambriæ.*   Lib. ii.,
cap i., and Camden in his description of Pembrokeshire.

† The valley in which Kilmune monastery lay abounded in
marble, and possibly the church or house had been built of this
material; so that it might be called *marmorea*, rather than *Rosea*
or *Rosina*, says Giraldus; for roses do not flourish there, while
marble is found in great abundance.

‡ See, *Acta Sanctorum Hiberniæ, Martii* 1. *Vita S. Davidis*,
n. 4, p. 430. This opinion he endeavours further to sustain, in
his Acts of Nennius or Monenennius, at the same day; but, I
think with no very successful result. See, *Ibid.* p. 439.

St. David was brought up at a place variously called, Vetus-Rubus, or Vetus-Menevia,* in Latin, and Henmenen in the Welsh language. He was there instructed in letters and ecclesiastical discipline. He was often discovered by his companions in the state of being taught by a dove, which warbled hymns with him. Hence, and for a reason to which allusion will be made hereafter, the pictures and statues of St. David usually represent him preaching on a hill, with a dove perched on his shoulder.† This bird, also, serves to typify the Holy Ghost, shedding the sweet influence of holy innocence and Divine Grace into his soul. Thus, our Saint grew

---

* This monastery seems to have borne no less than five distinct names, besides other forms of spelling. "Sortitus est autem locus hcc nomen ab Hibernico Muni," says Giraldus Cambrensis, "quod et Rubus sonat, unde et Kilmune Hibernice adhuc hodie Ecclesia Menevensis appellatur." See, *Acta Sanctorum Martii.* *Tomus* i. *Martii* 1. *Vita S. Davidis,* cap. i. *and* n. (n.) p. 42. Giraldus was well acquainted with its local characteristics. This Vitus Rubus appears to have differed from the new Menevia, to which St. David transferred his episcopal see, although it was identical with old Menevia. This latter, however, must have been situated, not very far from the present city, St. David's, and it was the site of an older religious house, in which our saint received his early rudiments of instruction.

† See, *Very Rev. F. C. Husenbeth's Emblems of Saints,* p. 45. As authority for this representation, he quotes Jacques Callot's *Les Images de tous les Saints et Saintes de l'année.* This latter work has been published in Paris, A.D. 1636. It contains engravings by Isr. Henriet.

in amiability and virtue, beloved by the children of men, and favoured specially by the Lord of Heaven.

Some persons supposed St. Patrick to have been the first founder of a monastery at Menevia, and that it had been afterwards restored or enlarged by St. David, about the year 490.* About this time, also, St. Finian of Clonard† is said to have left Ireland for Britain, where he formed an acquaintanceship and a friendship, with St. David.‡ At such date, as St. Benedict had been only a boy ten years old, it is not true that his rule had been then followed in Menevia.§

What has been evolved from contemporaneous incidents, when St. David flourished, shows St. Finnian of Clonard,‖ although he might have been a

---

* See, Bollandists' *Acta Sanctorum Martii. Tomus* i. *Vita S. Davidis*, p. 40. And Ussher's *Britannicarum Ecclesiarum Antiquitates*, cap. xiii. p. 253. Also *Index Chronologicus*, A.D. ccccxc., p. 524.

† See, Colgan's Acts of this saint, at the 23rd day of February. But the Bollandist editor says, this life had been edited from a Codex MS. of theirs, which wanted some correction.

‡ See, Ussher's *Britannicarum Ecclesiarum Antiquitates*, cap. xvii. p. 473, and *Index Chronologicus* ad A.D. ccccxi.

§ Edward Maihew, Bucelin, and other writers, say, that St. David followed the rule of St. Benedict.

‖ Finnian is not mentioned in any of St. David's lives. In his own Acts, when spoken of, as connected with David, he does not appear as a disciple. See, *Colgan's Acta Sanctorum Hiberniæ*, xxiii. *Februarii. Vita S. Finniani*, cap. iv. v. vi. vii. viii. ix. x. xi. pp. 393, 394.

companion in Britain, could hardly have been St. David's disciple. The holy bishop of Menevia was then too young to have been master over a man, who returned to Ireland, before the year 520. In all probability, Finnian was older than St. David. Still a learned Irish historian is inclined to think, that both studied together, at least during part of their scholarship, in some eminent British school. Such conclusion appears uncontravened by any existing record.

CHAPTER III.

St. David educated at first by Iltutus.—Afterwards instructed by Paulinus.—Ordained a priest.—Restores Paulinus to the use of sight.—Observations concerning Iltutus and Paulinus.

Our saint received his education at the school of Iltutus.* Afterwards, he studied with Paulinus,† it is thought, at Ty-gwyn-ar Dâf,‡ where he spent ten years in reading the Holy Scriptures. St. Ailbe,

---

* This school of Iltutus, at Laniltult, or Lantwitt, in Glamorganshire, is said to have been very celebrated, about the beginning of the sixth century. See Ussher's *Index Chronologicus* at A.D. 508, and Stillingfleet's *Antiquities of the British Churches*, chap. v. A Life of Iltutus mentions David, by mistake, as his scholar. The Bollandists and Stillingfleet observe, however, instead of David, we must read Daniel. This latter studied under Iltutus. Afterwards, he became first bishop of Bangor.

† According to Ussher's *Primordia*, p. 472, and Stillingfleet's *History of the British Churches*, there had been a school of Paulinus at Withland or Whiteland, in Caermarthen, and not the isle of Wight, as some have made it, in which St. David spent some of his early years. See his *Acts at the First of March*, cap. 8. Paulinus is said to have been a disciple of Iltutus. Considering the period, at which Iltutus's school was in vogue, Paulinus could scarcely have opened his before A.D. 512. See Dr. Lanigan's *Ecclesiastical History of Ireland*, vol. i., chap. ix., § ix., and note 151, pp. 471, 475, 476.

‡ In Caermarthenshire. "Below Talcharn the river *Taf* runs into the sea; on whose banks stood formerly the famous *Twy Gwin ar Taf* or *the White House on the Taf*, built of white hazel rods for a summer residence, where A.D. 914 Hoel surnamed the

who baptised him, is also said to have superintended his education, for some time.* Hence, we are supposed to obtain an additional proof, that David must have been very young, about the commencement of the sixth century.

He afterwards withdrew from all worldly allurements, and was ordained priest. He then began his missionary labours, and grounded well in exercises of piety, he preserved a chastened spirit, in the pursuit of greater learning and perfection. He set out for the Isle of Whiteland, Withland, or Witland,† where St. Paulinus,‡ a disciple to St. Ger-

---

Goad, prince of Wales, held an assembly, whereat assisted 140 ecclesiastics, besides others, and abrogating the ancient laws he enacted new ones for his people as the preamble to these laws sets forth. On this spot was afterwards built a monastery called *White Land*."—Gough's Camden's *Britannia*, p. 505.

* Usher makes such a statement from St. Ailbe's Life. See, *Primordia*, p. 871.

† Giraldus Cambrensis says, he set out, "In Vectam insulam." Camden tells us, the Anglo-Saxons called it Wuidland, or Withland, whilst the Britons named it Guith. In Caermarthen, ascribed to old Demetia, Whiteland was known by the Latin designation Albalandia, where a magnificent Cistercian monastery was built, regarding which a charter of King John exists. See, *Monasticon Anglicanum*, p. 884 et seq. This lay near Glamorgan, where Iltutus opened his school. Whiteland is mistaken for the Isle of Wight, by the learned Alban Butler, in his Life of St. David, at the 1st of March. See, *Lives of the Fathers, Martyrs and other Principal Saints*, vol. iii.

‡ By Capgrave, he is called, Paulentus or Poulentus.

manus, lived in a very holy manner. This distinguished teacher had been deprived of sight. Calling his disciples together, Paulinus ordered each in turn to offer a prayer and then to make a sign of the cross over his eyes. All obeyed these injunctions without any healing result, until David was called. This truly modest and humble young priest, by a religious habit acquired, constantly kept his eyes fixed on the ground. "Hitherto," said he, "I have not seen the face of my master." "Then," replied Paulinus, "touch my eyes, that I may behold thee!" David obeyed and sight was restored to his beloved master. However, such was the extraordinary abnegation and modesty of our saint, that for ten years sojourn with Paulinus, he never allowed his eyes to gaze upon the features of his holy director.*

In assuming Paulinus to have been the master of David, it is thought by Colgan, the former must have acted in his capacity as teacher to our saint, before the end of the fifth century. Ussher's opinion would seem to be, that David,—having been already promoted to the priesthood—studied under Paulinus, at the very commencement of the sixth century, and that he was a fellow-disciple about this time with Theliaus.† However, vainly endeavouring to identify

---

* See, *Colgan's Acta Sanctorum Hiberniæ*, 1 *Martii. Vita S. Davidis*, cap. vi. vii. viii., p. 426.

† See, at the year 500, Ussher's *Index Chronologicus*. It is

this Paulinus,* master of St. David, with others
bearing a similar name, Colgan is forced to a conclusion, that he may have been Hildutus or Iltutus,†
especially from one or two circumstances related regarding this latter saint. The first of these is, that
in David's life, published by himself, there is mention made concerning St. Paulinus and no word
about St. Iltutus, as our saint's teacher ; likewise,
in a life of this latter, which he cites, David, with
others, is said to have been taught by Iltutus.‡ In
the second place, as by the Rothe MS., by Cap-

___

strange, Colgan should cite Ussher, as naming A.D. 484, for this
course of instruction, more than once. He then infers from it,
that a certain St. Paulus, who died, A.D. 600 or 620, could not
have been the Paulinus, who was David's teacher, A.D. 484.
Ussher has no such account. St. Paulus, called Leonensis Episcopus, is said to have been a disciple of Iltutus, and to have died at
Bath, more than one hundred years old, A.D. 600, according to
Claudius Roberti, in *Catalogus Episcoporum Leonensium*, at this
year. Ussher also places his death about the same time, in his
Index Chronologicus; but in the body of his work, adds, " vel
etiam DCXX. pervenisse traditur," and for this latter date he cites
John Capgrave, after *Vita S. Ithamari.* See, *Britannicarum
Ecclesiarum Antiquitates*, cap. xiv. p. 290.

* Giraldus says: " tandem Paulinus episcopus, cum quo David
olim liberalibus disciplinis in pueritia studuerat." From this it is
not easy to determine, whether Paulinus was the master or fellow-
disciple of St. David.

† Capgrave gives his acts, and tells us, he was venerated on the
viii. of the Ides of November.

‡ Speaking about this saint, his life has it, that many scholars

grave,* and by Giraldus,† Paulinus is called a disciple of St. Germanus, the Bishop; so, according to another authority, St. Iltutus is said to have been a disciple of the same Germanus.‡ And lastly, St. Paulinus, together with David, Dubricius, Daniel and others, is reported to have assisted at the Synod of Brevi,§ held in the country of Ceretica. Now,

---

flocked to him, "quorum de numero quatuor isti, Samson, Paulinus, Gildas, et Dewi, id est, David studebant sapienter." Here, Paulinus or Paulus is represented as a fellow-disciple of St. David. Colgan tells us, he who in the Life of Iltutus is titled Paulinus, should rather be regarded as "Paulus episcopus Oxismorum sive Leonensis." This would appear, from a Life of St. Gildas, in *Bibliotheca Floriacensi*, where Gildas, Paulus Leonensis and Samson are enumerated amongst the disciples of Hiltutus. How is it likely, we may ask, that the master and disciple, bearing different names, could have been mistaken for one and the same person? There was another St. Paulinus, Bishop of Capua, who lived about A.D. 570, according to Ferrarius, *De Sanctis Italiæ*; and Baronius, in his notes to the Martyrology, at the 10th of October. Colgan, however, adds regarding him: "Sed an in Britanniam venerit, vel institutor S. Davidis usque ad annum 570 pervenerit, nullo mihi argumento constat."

* Capgrave calls him Paulentus.

† Giraldus names him Paulinus. It is not reasonable to suppose, he could be identical with St. Paulinus, Apostle of Northumbria, and Archbishop of York, who died A.D. 640. See his life at the 10th of October, the day of his feast, in Rev. Alban Butler's *Lives of the Fathers, Martyrs and other Principal Saints*, vol. x.

‡ Vincentius, *In Speculo Hystoriali*. Lib. xx. cap. 105, and *Vita S. Samsonis*, preserved in a Landaff Registry.

§ A.D. 519, according to Ussher. See, *Britannicarum Ecclesi-*

St. Iltutus is supposed to have flourished about the same time, in this region. It is not likely, he was absent from such an important Synod, writes Colgan; or if present, that he had been omitted from that account, contained in the Rothe MS.* The author, who wrote this Life of St. David, seems to have supposed, that the person, called by him Paulinus, had been named Iltutus, by other writers.† Indeed, it becomes no easy matter to determine this question with perfect accuracy.

---

arum Antiquitates, cap. xiii., pp. 253, 254, and *Index Chronologicus ad ann. DXIX.,* p. 526.

* The only inference to be drawn from such a statement is, that under the title Paulinus must also be understood a personal identity with St. Iltutus.

† Our Irish hagiologist adds:— "Alias cur aileret disoipulatum apud Iltutum, virum origine Britannum et inter Britannos notissimum, memorato ejus discipulatu apud Paulinum Britannicis scriptorlbus ignotum, si a Paulino sit diversus." See, *Acta Sanctorum Hiberniæ,* 1 *Martii. Vita S. Davidis,* n. 10, p. 431.

CHAPTER IV.

St. David admonished by an Angel to commence his mission.—
Restores Glastonbury.—Builds a chapel in honour of the
Blessed Virgin Mary.—King Ina's foundations for Irish students.—Death and burial of King Arthur.—Religious erection
at Bath by St. David.—He blesses the springs at this place.

WHEN David had spent a sufficient length of time
with Paulinus, the Angel of the Lord said to this
latter holy man : " It is time that God's beloved—
a talent entrusted to thy care—should be presented
for the salvation of souls." And the works of our
saint soon became manifested to men. He founded
or re-edified no less than twelve monasteries. Among
these, one of the most celebrated was known as
Glastonbury, on the confines of Somersetshire. However, we are not to regard St. David, as the original
founder, but rather as the rebuilder or restorer of
this ancient religious establishment.* For we even

* St. Joseph of Arimathea, with his disciples, is said to have
settled in this place, and to have consecrated it. Afterwards, St.
Fagan, St. David, St. Patrick, with innumerable other holy and
learned men, are found connected with this celebrated monastery.
Ussher cites the following Latin verses, taken from an old
chronicle :

> " Intrat Avalloniam duodena caterva virorum ;
> Flos Arimatheæ Joseph est primus eorum.
> Josephes ex Joseph genitus patrem comitatur ;
> His aliisque decem jus Glastoniæ propriatur."

See, *Britannicarum Ecclesiarum Antiquitates*, cap. ii. p. 8. Also
cap. vi. p. 55.

learn, from an ancient local chronicle, that when Archbishop of Caerleon on Usk, St. David,* with seven bishops, over whom he presided, visited Glastonbury.† There he made arrangements, for dedicating its old church, in honour of the Blessed Virgin Mary. Another record, in nearly similar terms, assigns this dedication to the year preceding.‡ Yet, in a more modern work, it is stated, that at a still earlier period, about A.D. 530,§ St. David and his suffragan bishops laid out vast sums in adding to and adorning buildings belonging to this monastery. The town itself is situated in Somersetshire, or the Isle of Avalon,‖ which has been also called Inis Witrin, or the Glassy Island.

---

* Our Saint is there called " Legionum archiepiscopus." Under the year of grace 516, we read, " Dubritius urbis Legionum Archiepiscopus," in Matthew of Westminster. See *Flores Historiarum*, p. 185.

† This visit has been assigned to A.D. 566. A tablet at Glastonbury placed it at 565. But these dates are subsequent to the year generally assigned for our Saint's death.

‡ See, Ussher's *Britannicarum Ecclesiarum Antiquitates*, cap. v. p. 47. This learned writer places the work of restoration under the year 529. See *Index Chronologicus*, p. 528.

§ See, *Britannia ; or, A Chronographical Description of the Flourishing Kingdoms of England, Scotland and Ireland, and the Islands adjacent, from the earliest antiquity. By William Camden. Translated from the edition published by the Author in MDCVII. Enlarged by the latest discoveries, by Richard Gough, F.A. & R.L.S.* Vol. i. p. 58, note (u.)

‖ It is said to have been so called, because it produced good

This latter name, it is supposed, must have been derived, from the *glasten* or blueish-green colour of its earthy surface ; or, because the aborigines here found an herb, known as *glast*, or *woad*, which served to tinge their bodies. This town, like many others, is indebted for its origin, to early monastic institutions.* Indeed, many houses, in the present town of Glastonbury, are built entirely of stones, taken from the remains of its once magnificent monastery.

From a certain old record,† we learn, that when St. David came to Glastonbury, he intended to dedicate the church, already restored, to nearly its former appearance. Yet, the Lord miraculously appeared to him in sleep, and dissuaded him from this purpose.‡ Being warned by a Divine revela-

---

apples. In the British and Irish language, *Auall* is said to mean *an* apple.

* See, *The Beauties of England and Wales ; or Original De-lineations, Topographical, Historical, and Descriptive of each County. Embellished with engravings.* Vol. xiii. Part i. pp. 494, 499. This article on Glastonbury, compiled by the Rev. J. Nightingale, is illustrated by three exquisite copperplate engravings, representing its antiquities. The History of Glastonbury is a very interesting one. Some of the Abbey ruins exhibit the former glories of this place.

† Such account is contained in a MS. History of Glastonbury church, preserved in the Cotton Library. See, *Monasticon Anglicanum.* Vol. i. p. 1.

‡ The account adds: "Necnon in signum quod Dominus ipse

tion, St. David added another minor chapel, in form of a chancel, to the eastern side of this church. This he consecrated, in honour of the Blessed Virgin Mary; and to commemorate still more such an event, he brought a precious altar of his own to the place. That posterity might know at what point the chapel had been united to the church, a pyramid was exteriorly erected, towards the North; and an inner grade or line facing the South, showed the place where St. Joseph, with a great number of saints, had been buried, according to the opinion of some antiquarians. This place became a sepulchre in after time, for kings, queens, bishops, and nobles. The chapel was consequently held in great veneration, and it was munificently endowed.*

In a charter of Ina, king over the East Saxons, several hides of land, with other privileges and possessions, are enumerated, as having been bestowed on this old chapel† of the Blessed Virgin.

Ecclesiam ipsam prius cum ejus Cimiterio dedicaverat, manum Episcopi digito perforavit; Et sic perforata multis videntibus in crastino apparuit."

* Views of Glastonbury town and its ancient ruins are to be seen appended to the foregoing account, in *Monasticon Anglicanum* Vol. i. p. 3.

† Before particularising the several donatives to this establishment, it is parenthetically remarked: " Quam magnus Sacerdos a Pontifex summus Anglorem Christus obsequio, sibi ac perpetuae Virgini Mariae, et beato David, multis et inauditis miraculis olim se sanctificasse innotuit." See, *Spelman's Concilia*, pp. 227, 228.

These were intended for the use of Glastonbury monks, who had practised there a life of regular observance. The date of this charter has been assigned to A.D. 725.*

It was traditionally held, that when the little ancient church, said to have been here built by Joseph of Arimathea, fell into decay, David, bishop of St. David's, erected a new one, on the same spot. This structure appears to have been evanescent as the former;† for, it became ruinous in a short time. It was next rebuilt by twelve persons, from the northern parts of Britain. Even this latter church did not last; for King Ina had it pulled down, towards the close of the seventh or commencement of the eighth century. He then built a magnificent one, which was dedicated in honour of Christ, under the invocation of his two glorious Apostles, SS. Peter and Paul, as an inscription in elegiac Latin verse on its upper cornice testified.‡ In those early times, men of most exemplary lives, " especially the Irish," as we are informed, devoted themselves to a religious life. They were maintained at the King's expense, while engaged instructing youth in

---

* See *Ibid.* p. 227.

† It was probably built of wood or planks, and consequently no trace of it can be found at present.

‡ This inscription, with a versified English translation, is to be found in *Gough's Camden's Britannia.* Vol. i. pp. 58, 59.

the principles of religion, in practices of piety, and in acquisition of the liberal sciences.* Even many

---

* One of the St. Patricks from Ireland—known as St. Patrick senior—A.D. 435, here gathered the first regular congregation of monks. Here likewise he lived thirty years as a monk, and he was buried on the north side of the altar. See, *Ibid.*, and William of Malmsbury's *History and Antiquities of Glastonbury*, printed in folio, by Gale, at Oxford, A.D. 1691. Here, also, died and was interred the renowned King Arthur—said to have been St. David's nephew—on the 21st of May, A.D. 542. According to a bardic tradition, Speed relates, that his body was deposited between two *Pyramids*, standing in the churchyard of Glastonbury. King Henry II. of England "caused the ground to be digged, and at seven foot depth was found a huge broad stone, wherein a Leaden Crosse was fastened, and in that side that lay downward, in rude and barbarous letters (as rudely set and contrived) this inscription written vpon that side of the Lead that was towards the stone." There is an engraving of this lead cross, with an inscription, in very ancient lettering, given: HIC JACET SEPULTUS INCLITUS REX ARTURIUS IN INSULA AVALONIA. The cross of lead and its inscription had been long preserved in the Treasury or Register of Glastonbury church, until the time of Henry VIII., according to Stowe. The body of Queen Gueneucr, Arthur's wife, was found beside his own. Both were enclosed in the trunk of a Tree, nine feet below the "huge broad stone." Ten wounds were traceable on the skull of King Arthur. Finely platted tresses, in colour like gold, remained on the queen's skull. On being touched, these latter turned into dust. Of this exhumation, Giraldus Cambrensis was an eye-witness. "The bones of King *Arthur* and of Queen *Guineuer*, his wife, by the direction of *Henry de Bloys*, Nephew to King *Henry* the Second, and Abbat of *Glastenbury*, at that present, were translated into the great new church, and there in a faire Tombe of Marble, his body was laid, and his *Queenes* at his feete; which noble Monument among the fatall

of these students led solitary lives, that they might
have greater leisure for learned pursuits, and greater
opportunities for the practice of asceticism and
mortification.* Owing to such circumstances, this
place received the title, Glas-nan Geadhel, or *Glassia
Hibernorum*, in Latin; for it became a favourite
place of resort for our countrymen, many of whom
rendered it still more celebrated, by their piety,
learning and residence. Amongst them, various
saints are enumerated.†

---

overthrowes of infinite more, was altogether raced at the dispose
of some then in commission; whose too forward zeale, and ouer-
hasty actions in these behalfes, hath left vnto vs a want of many
truths, and cause to wish that some of their imployments had
beene better spent."—See Speed's *Historie of Great Britaine.*
Booke vii. chap. xii. pp. 272, 273.

  * See, *Gough's Camden's Britannia*

  † The principal one of these was St. Patrick Senior, to whom
Marianus Gorman alludes in his Martyrology, at the 24th of
August, in these words: " S. Patricius Senex in Ros-dela in regione de Magh-lacha, et in Glais na ngaehdel, id est, Glassiæ Hibernorum, quæ est urbs in Aquilonari regione Saxonum : in qua
olim suscepta peregrinatione solebant Hiberni habitare: ejus antem
reliquiæ jacent in reliquiario Senioris Patricii Ardmachiæ." And
the calendar of Cashel, at the same day, has the following account: "Patricius senior quiescit in Ros dela in regione Mag-
lacha quiescit. Sed secundum aliquos, et verius, Glastoniæ
Hibernorum quiescit senior Patricius. Hæc enim est civitas in
Aquilonari regione Saxonum, et Scoti habitant eam. Ejus autem
reliquiæ jacent in reliquiario S. Patricii Ardmachiæ." The Martyrologies of St. Ængus, Maguire and Donegall, as we are told,

We read, that King Arthur,* having been mor-
tally wounded by Modred,† in Cornubia, near the
river Kemelen, in the year of our Lord 542, had
been brought to the Island of Avallon, that his

---

have similar accounts, regarding this St. Patrick Senior, at the
24th of August. However, in *The Martyrology of Donegall,*
published by Drs. Todd and Reeves, I find no mention regarding
him, at the date in question.

* He is said to have been the son of Nazaleod or Uther, and to
have succeeded him, A.D. 514. Many fabulous and romantic
things have been related, concerning this renowned champion of
the British nation. He powerfully resisted the Pagan Saxons;
but, whether he was king of the Britons in general, or only a
Prince over Cornwall, is uncertain. See, Echard's *History of
England.* Vol. i. book i. chap. ii. cent. vi. p. 41. In another a -
count, I find Uter "called *Pendragon,* of his Royal Banner born
ever before him; wherein was pourtrayed a Dragon with a Golden
Head, as in our *English* camps it is at this day born for the
Imperial Standard."—Sir Richard Baker's *Chronicle of the Kings
of England,* p. 4. By the same author, we are told, that Arthur
was son "of the fair Lady Igren;" but, we may well doubt the
veracity of this account, as it has been connected with a fabulous
and an absurd tradition.

† In *Polydori Vergilii Urbinatis Anglicæ Historiæ Libri Vigin-
tiseptem.* Lib. iii. p. 60, this enemy cf King Arthur is called
"Mordredum nepotem." He is said to have excited insurrection,
during the king's absence on a warlike expedition having the city
of Rome for its object. Mordred is also said to have been killed
in this battle. Polydore Virgil was born about A.D. 1470, and he
died in 1555. See notices regarding him and his writings in the
*Biographie Universelle, Ancienne et Moderne, cr. Redigé par une
Société de Gens de Lettres et de Savants.* Tome xxxv. pp. 260,
261, 262.

wound might be healed. Here he died, and was buried in the cemetery of the monks, during summer, and about the feast of Pentecost. His queen Guenevera was interred beside him. We are told, they rested in their grave for 648 years, when their remains were afterwards removed to the larger church.* Immediately before the death of Arthur, in 542, he is said to have bequeathed his British crown to a kinsman, named Constantine, son to Cador, chief of Cornubia. Then, we are informed, the most holy Archbishop of Caerleon, David, died in his city of Menevia, and within the Abbey, which he loved more than all the other religious houses in his diocese. This was because, it had been founded by St. Patrick, who predicted his own nativity.† Whilst sojourning in this monastery with his *confrères*, a sudden weakness, betokening the approach of death, came over him. By order of Malgon, king of the Venedoti, he was buried in the Church

---

* The foregoing account is set down in some ancient records of Glastonbury church. See *Monasticon Anglicanum*. Vol. i. p. 7. The writers of British History, who confirm this statement, are Thomas Rodburn, Walter of Oxford, Geoffrey of Monmouth, Matthew of Westminster, Alan Insulensis, and the Annals of Winton monastery. Amongst Scottish writers, are John Fordun, John Major, and Hector Boetius, who accord in their several works. These are cited and followed by Ussher.

† Here, evidently, the popular tradition has confounded the great Apostle of Ireland, with a St. Patrick, designated Senior.

of Menevia. Then, after giving an account of Constantine's wars, it is said he was killed by Conan,
in the third year of his reign,* which must have
been, A.D. 545.†

Another recorded religious foundation effected by
St. David was at Bath,‡ in Somersetshire. Here,
we are told, that owing to his blessing, water which
heretofore had proved most deleterious to health
became afterwards most salubrious to persons washed

---

* Godfrey, or Geoffrey, of Monmouth gives the foregoing account in his Chronicle. Lib. ii. cap. 2, 3, 4.

† Such, at least, is the inference of the Bollandist editor, who
says: "recte erui infra ex Vita, num. 17. mortuum esse anno
intermedio DXLIV, quo cyclo solis XXI, litteris Dominicalibus
CB, Kalendæ Martiæ in feriam tertiam convenere : qui obitus ejus
characteres ibidem observantur." See, *Acta Sanctorum Martii.*
Tomus i. *Martii* 1, *Vita S. Davidis. Commentarius Prævius.* § ii.
n. 14, pp. 40, 41.

‡ The name, in the original account, is Badum. Camden has
a description concerning it, in his account of Somersetshire. See
Colgan's *Acta Sanctorum Hiberniæ,* 1 *Martii. Vita S. Davidis.*
§ ix. p. 426, and n. 13, p. 431, *Ibid.* Also, *Gough's Camden's
Britannia,* where it is described, as lying on the noble river Avon.
It is an antient city "called by Ptolemy from its baths, Ὕδατα
Θερμα, or the *Warm Waters,* by Antoninus AQUÆ SOLIS, by the
Britons *Yr ennaint twymin* and *Caer Badon,* by the Saxons,
Bathancester, Hat Bathan, and from the resort of the sick *Akeman-
cester,* q.d. the city of the sick; by Stephanus *Badiza,* by us at
present *Bathe,* and in modern Latin *Bathonia.* It stands in a
small plain, fenced as it were on every side by hills of equal
height, from whence perpetual springs descend into the city to the
great convenience of the inhabitants." See vol. i. p. 61.

by it.* Whether, this account has any reference to the famous Thermal and warm water fountains, so well known and so long resorted to by invalids, we have no means left for ascertaining. But, there is every reason for supposing such identification.† These appear to have been known from the most remote antiquity. Yet, we can find no very satisfactory account, regarding the religious foundation of St. David, at this place. Probably, the materials used in its construction were not destined for a durability, greater than had been effected in the case of Glastonbury. In all likelihood, it perished, during the destructive wars waged at this period of British history.

---

* See Tanner's *Notitia Monastica; or an Account of All the Abbies, Priories and Houses of Friers, formerly in England and Wales,* edited by James Nasmith, M.A., Somersetshire. V. Bath, n. (k). This erudite and valuable edition is without any paging.

† We are informed by a modern Protestant historian, that " giving to the *Bath-waters* the virtues they still retain" is one of those miracles attributed to St. David. See, Rapin de Thoyra's *History of England.* Vol. i. book ii. p. 43. Translated by N. Tindal, M.A.

CHAPTER V.

Missionary works undertaken by St. David, during the Saxon incursions.—Condition of Wales about this period.—Restored sight of King Ertig.—An angelic monition.—Many disciples flock to St. David.—Opposition experienced, and the designs of Pagan enemies frustrated.

MANY other monasteries were erected by our Saint.* Yet, these religious works seem to have been undertaken and executed, at a time, when social disturbances prevailed over a great portion of Britain.† The Picts, Scots and Saxons had already made inroads on the disunited aboriginal inhabitants. In 449,

---

* In addition to those already named, the Utrecht MS. says: "Postea Caulam et Reptum, Coluam et Glastum, deinde Seumnistre, postea Raclam: hinc Langhemalach, in quo postea altare missum accepit." We are told, by the Bollandist editor, that these seven monasteries have been omitted, by other writers; probably, because they had ceased to exist, at the period of their writing. Two additional monasteries are named by Capgrave: "Lemustir et aliud in Govvir in Wallia." But, perhaps, the first may be regarded as identical with "Secumnistre." In the text of Giraldus Cambrensis, we read: "Postea Croulam et Reptum, Colvan et Glascum. Ex hinc Leonis monasterium, Ragalan quoque in Winta, et Langevelach apud Goer, ubi et altare missum a Domino postea suscepit."—*Lect.* iii. Ricemarc has *Repetun*, for Reptum; *Colyuan*, for Colvan; Leuministre for Leonis; *Raglam in regione Guent* for Ragalan; and *Guhir* for Goer.

† I know of no other work more elegantly and learnedly written, on the history of this early period, or ages subsequent

the Saxons first landed, as pretended auxiliaries of
the Britons, on the Isle of Thanet. But, they soon
found or sought a pretext for quarrelling with their
allies. The Saxon invasion of England levelled
churches and monasteries of the conquered Britons ;
whilst Paganism and barbarism triumphed over the
early victories of Christianity in Southern England.
The two last bishops of these vanquished Britons
abandoned their churches and pastoral charges of
London and York, in 586. Carrying with them
relics of saints and consecrated vessels, they followed
tribes of their people and race, seeking refuge west-
wards amongst the inaccessible mountains of Wales.*
The Saxons now dreamed only of conquest, and an
unrelenting struggle continued, almost without inter-
mission, for a period of one hundred and fifty years.
Indeed, it never entirely ceased, until the warlike
Saxon finally yielded to the hardy and enterprising
Danes and Normans, in the eleventh century. Wales
had its part in these internecine contests ;† but, the

---

thereto, and which will give the reader more accurate accounts
than Sharon Turner's *History of the Anglo-Saxons*, in four
volumes, 8vo. This work was first published in London, at the
close of the last, and beginning of the present century.

* See, Le Comte de Montalembert's work, *Les Moines d'
Occident, depuis Saint Benoit jusqu' à Saint Bernard.* Tome iii.
livre x. xii.

† See that valuable and compendious work, the Rev. Thomas
Flanogan's *Manual of British and Irish History, illustrated with*

early history of this province requires further eluci-
dation, from its numerous records yet existing.*

This remarkable division of Britain, now for many
ages past united to England, had been called " Britannia Secunda" under Roman rule. Formerly, it
had been governed by its own rulers. When the
Anglo-Saxons occupied most other parts of Britain,
and had given different names to kingdoms founded
by them, many people, retaining the name of Britons,
fled into Wales, so that they might not dwell with
the idolatrous Anglo-Saxons. In Wales, they lived
under the rule of petty kings. Afterwards, it is
said, to have been named Cambria, or even, as many

---

*Maps, Engravings, and Statistical, Chronological and Genealogical
Tables.* Chap. i. p. 18, chap. ii. p. 21. There we read : " Some
maintain that the inhabitants of Wales are not ancient Britons
but Picts. Their principal reasons are, that the Welsh have not
retained the old name Silures and Ordovices ; that the genealogies
of their principal families almost invariably lead back to the
Pictish kingdom of Strathclyde, or the Valley of the Clyde; and
that the language of the Picts, if we may judge from one or two
words that remain, was decidedly Welsh. These reasons, however, are not in themselves conclusive, and they take it for granted
that the Picts were a different race from the ancient Britons, a
position by no means substantiated, and generally denied." See
Ibid. p. 24, note.

* " The Welsh language affords upwards of a thousand, we will
venture to say two thousand manuscripts of very considerable
antiquity." See, *The Mgvyrian Archiaology of Wales.* Vol. i.
Preface.

think, this had been its original denomination. It
is still poetically known by this latter name. Among
the people of Armoric Gaul and those Britons very
friendly relations existed. The Armoric district was
even called Britain, by the Gauls; whilst the other
Britain or Cambria had been designated Gualla and
then Wallia. This was supposed to have been derived from the name of Gaul.* Such derivation
appears more probable than one offered by an old
English chronicler, that Wales took its appellation
from a Princess named Walia.†

After giving an account of St. David's various
religious foundations, the Utrecht MS. relates, that
he restored sight to a King Ertig,‡ who was a relation

---

* See *Acta Sanctorum Martii. Tomus* i. *Martii. Vita S.
Davidis. Commentarius Prævius.* § i. n. i. p. 38.

† Du Chesne, in his *Histoire Generale d'Angleterre, D'Ecosse,
et D'Irlande, Livre* v. p. 263, after giving an account of the dis-
persion into Armorica, adds: "Les autres qui cherchcrent une
patrie dedans leur propre patrie, se refug'erent és pays appellez
depuis et maintenent encor par les Anglois *Walles*, ou Galles, &
Cornwal. Appellations derivées du mot *Welsh*, ou *Walsh*, c'est
à dire estranger & d'autre nation, entre les Germains. Car quant
a ceux qui les ont voulu tirer des Gaulois, comme Bucanan, ou
d'une Princesse appellee Walia, comme Geofroy de Moumoulth,
il semble que leurs conjectures sont foibles, & sans aucun fon-
dement."

‡ He is called, "Ergin cui nomen Proprius," by Giraldus.
Lect. iii. Ricemarc has it, "Pepiau regem Erging."

of his own.* Having established the cenobitical rule, in houses of his appointment, he prepared for a return to the place, whence he had set out, namely Menevia, and there Bishop Duisdianus† lived. Here, while conversing together on pious topics and in a friendly manner, they proposed remaining. But an Angel said in their hearing: "Scarcely one in a hundred shall enjoy Heavenly rewards, in the place where you purpose serving God. But near this, there is another spot," showing Rossina valley,‡ "and of those who shall be buried in its cemetery, scarcely one shall suffer the pains of hell, provided they fall not from the faith."§

In a short time, the celebrity of St. David, as a master of the spiritual life, spread abroad, throughout his own country and in more distant lands. Soon, many disciples began to collect around him. Among these, we find the Irish Saint Moedoc or Aidan,

---

* Here Ricemarc interposes: "Duo quoque sancti Boducat et Maitrun in provincia Celgueli dederunt sibi manus."

† Giraldus writes: "Erat autem eodem tempore ibidem episcopus avunculus ejus, vir venerabilis, cui nomen Gistlianus." In another account, we have, " Giustilianus fratruelis ejus."

‡ Ricemarc adds: "Quem vulgari nomine Hoduant Britones vocitant." Giraldus adds: "ubi sacrum hodie cimiterium extat, longe religioni et sanctæ congregationi competentior. Ex hoc nempe maximos sibi divina providentiā fidelium animarum thesauros elegit." *Lect.* iii.

§ See, *Acta Sanctorum Martii. Tomus* i. *Martii.* i. *Vita S. Davidis.* Cap. ii. § 5, p. 42.

afterwards bishop of Ferns,* St. Eliud,† who is called, also, Teilo, Theliaus, Teilaus, Teilanus or

---

* His feast is celebrated in this diocese as a double of the First Class, and with an octave, on the 31st of January. Teilo is said to have been, not a disciple, but a fellow-disciple, with St. David. In the Utrecht MS., the names of saints, mentioned in the text, are not given.

† According to some writers, this saint immediately succeeded St. David, as bishop of Menevia. But, Giraldus Cambrensis tells us, that a Cenaucus or Kinocus was the immediate successor of our saint, and that after him came Eliud Teliau or Teilanus. See, *Itinerarium Cambriæ*. Lib. ii. cap. i. and *Vita S. Davidis*. Amongst the Charters of Donations granted by King Ido, son to Ynir Guent, as found in the Registry of Landaff, we find foremost the signatures of clergy, *Teliaus Archiepiscopus;* "ille nimirum," adds Ussher, "quem Davidi suo Menevenses, in sede vero Ladavensi Dubricio successisse alii tradiderunt." *Britannicarum Ecclesiarum Antiquitatis*. Cap. v. p. 52. As Teilo succeeded Dubricius, in the see of Landaff. it has been conjectured, that some error must have occurred in placing his name amongst the Archbishops of St. David's See.—*The Beauties of England and Wales, &c. South Wales. By Thomas Rees, F.S.A.* Vol. xviii. p. 847. Yet, his name, Eliud or Teilaus, is given as *third* in succession from St. David, in a list of Menevian bishops, drawn up by Giraldus; while, in another list, prepared by Godwin, on the authority of an ancient document, belonging to St. David's church, Eliud is represented as the *second* and Theliaus as the *third* bishop, succeeding our saint. See, *Ibid*. pp. 845, 846. Hence, to me, it does not seem clear, that Eliud was identical with Teilo. This latter, also, known as Teilaus or Teleanus, was venerated, we are told, at Landaff, in Glamorganshire, on the 25th of November. Here, it is said, he had been educated under St. Dubritius and St. David. As another saint, bearing this name, has not been discovered, Herman Greuen or the Carthusian Martyrology records his festival

Teleanus, together with Ismael. Regarding this latter, little appears to be known ; but according to some accounts, Ismael is represented as the immediate successor of St. David. Ismael is also said to have been a disciple of Dubricius, and to have been consecrated by Teilo. While these three saints, with other fellow-disciples, were one day in company, an Angel directed their course towards a place, where a fire was kindled. From this spot a column of smoke ascended. It seemed, not only to cover all the land of Britain, but it even enveloped the whole Island of Hibernia. We are told, that a certain inhabitant, named Boia, * living in that part of Wales, trembled when he witnessed this sign. He felt so

---

probably at the 9th of February. " In Britannia S. Teillani Confessoris." The English Martyrology does not make him a Confessor, but a Martyr. It says that he fell by the hand of a noble, called Gueddan, A.D. 626. Colgan remarks, that in the beginning of the seventh century a Saint Telleus or Telleanus, an Irishman, lived. He was descended from the family of Colla Dacrioch, as appears in the *Martyrologium Genealogicum*, cap. 12, and *Vita S. Munnæ*, cap. 10. He had been venerated at the church of Teghtelle, in Westmeath, on the 25th of June, as would appear from the Martyrologies of Tallagh, Marianus Gorman, Maguire and Donegall. But, until the Acts of this Telleus or Teilo, mentioned in the text, came into Colgan's hands, or some valid source of evidence became available, our Irish hagiologist would not pronounce for their identity or distinction. See, *Acta Sanctorum Hiberniæ*, 1 *Martii. Vita S. Davidis.* n. 16, pp. 431, 432.

* " Baia vocatus Scottus," says Ricemarc.

very much depressed in mind, that he spent the whole day in grief and fasting. When his wife asked the cause for his extraordinary depression of countenance and spirits, Boia replied to her: " I have seen a smoke arising from Rossina valley, covering, as it were, the whole land, and I fear the mystery it conceals. From this omen, I undoubtedly anticipate, that he, who hath lighted such a fire, must excel all other inhabitants of this land in power and glory." His wife, who participated in these prejudices of her husband, advised the latter to gather a number of his followers, and massacre those who had lighted the fire. Having prepared to obey these her instructions, six of his followers were seized with fever on the way. The rest of these retainers, finding their object could not be accomplished, returned, only to hear from Boia's wife, that their cattle had perished during their absence. On learning this news, they said one to another, " Let us go back, and on bended knees entreat God's servants to remove their ban from ourselves and from our cattle." This they did in all humility, confessing their fault and shedding an abundance of tears, whilst they said : " May the land in which you live belong to you for ever." St. David had compassion on them, and he affectionately told them, their animals should again come to life; and as he had promised, so it happened.

By other improper means, we are informed, Boia's

wife contrived to render this place of habitation*
distasteful to the monks, and they proposed that St.
David should abandon it. But their holy superior
said : " As, through many tribulations, persecutions
and continuous wars against seven nations, whose
destruction God had ordered, his Israelites came to
the Land of Promise ; so, at the present time, those
who desire rest in a heavenly country, must be exposed to many adversities, and yet not fail, but
valiantly resist every effort of the enemy, through
God's assistance. Be you therefore faithful, nor let
the enemy rejoice at your flight. For we must
remain, and Boia, with his wife, shall yield to us."
With such words, he fortified the minds of his disciples and rendered them inflexible in their purpose.
The very next day, Boia's wife lapsed into insanity,
nor did she ever recover from it.† Boia himself
soon perished, receiving an unexpected stroke from

---

* The place where St. David and his monks then lived is designated "Collegii Pænitentia," in the Utrecht MS. And to this
the editor has appended the following note: " *Albertus le Grand
in Vita S. Sezni eremetorium hujus Sancti Britannis ait vocari*
Peneti Sant Sezni : *et alibi insinuat pro* pœnitentiali *hanc vocem
accepi, id est, loco pænitentiæ exercendæ destinato ; fortassis hic
quoque rectius* Penetia, *seu* Pœnitentialia *legeretur.*" *Vita S.
Davidis.* Cap. ii. n. (e.) p. 43.

† The Utrecht MS. adds, to this account of Boia's wife:
" occisa prius innocenti privigna (in cujus martyrii sede fons sanita-
tum redditor emanavit)."

the hands of an enemy; a fire or lightning sent
from heaven burned his dwelling; and in these
visible judgments, the power of God was terribly
manifested.*

---

* See, *Colgan's Acta Sanctorum Hiberniæ.* 1 *Martii. Vita S.
Davidis.* §§. x. xi. p. 426.

CHAPTER VI.

St. David founds his monastery.—Rules there established for his monks.—Their observances and austere practices.—Personal example of our Saint—His preaching and perfect piety.

THROUGH Divine agency, his adversaries having been removed, St. David founded a very celebrated monastery, on that identical spot, pointed out by the Angel. He then commenced, by setting his house in order. He decreed, whatever his brethren might there acquire, by daily labour, should be appropriated for their common support. This holy man recognized the fact, proved by experience, that idleness is the source and origin of most vices. Therefore, did he require the monks to labour hard, each day; for he knew, that were they to rest entirely, a spirit of sloth or luxury must pervert their minds. He constantly set before them a necessity for labouring in earnest, so that the Devil might never find them idle. They must reject all presents and despise riches. Nor would he allow a yoke of oxen to plough their land; this work of tillage should be performed alone by manual labour. During their hours for toil, or when leaving off work for the day, he would not have a single unnecessary word or idle conversation amongst his disciples, who were then required to engage in prayer or holy meditation. When their hours for agricultural work had elapsed, these monks were enjoined to return to their monastery, where their remaining time until evening came was devoted to reading, writing and prayer. When evening came the sound of a bell was heard. Then each monk left his studies, and went in silence to the common place for assembling. At the very first stroke of this bell, when heard, each monk was obliged to rise instantly, nor dare he finish a single letter he had been writing. He must even leave it partially formed. When they had chaunted the Divine Office and Hymns, with great reverence, in the church ; his monks afterwards, on bended knees, made an examination of conscience, with much interior devotion, and often accompanied with penitential tears.

When these holy religious took food in a common refectory, it was through matter of necessity, and not to please the palate. Their rule required great abstemiousness. They were obliged to live on bread, vegetables and salt. They regarded any more generous food with aversion. But, in the case of infirm, aged or over-fatigued monks, better fare was sometimes very wisely allowed.

Having given thanks to God after meals, the monks entered church in their usual manner. Then during three hours, they were accustomed to kneel, to pray and to meditate. Whilst praying in church, they were forbidden to yawn, to cough or to spit; these being regarded as improprieties, quite unbecoming the sacred place, and occasion, for which they had assembled.

When all their daily exercises had ended, they prepared for nightly repose. That this was of brief duration would appear, from an account how they arose at cock-crow, again to engage in prayer and genuflexion. They were obliged to keep vigil until the dawn of morning. They were clad, likewise, in very coarse habits, chiefly formed from the skins of beasts.

His monks were accustomed to reveal their secret thoughts to their holy superior, and in the performance of most trivial things, they wished to secure his permission. Their monastic property was common to all, so that none of the brethren could say, "this is mine," or, "that is yours." Whoever infringed on the letter or spirit of this rule was subjected to a severe penance. They never failed in obedience to their superior's orders. Their single-mindedness was admirable, and their perseverance in action was a mark of their religious vocation. Whatever candidate for admission to this community presented himself, withdrawing from worldly engagements, was first required to remain ten days, before the door of the monastery. There he only heard reproachful and discouraging words addressed to him. If he had patience to bear such an ordeal for ten days, the postulant was received. Then he first served under a senior, appointed to this office for a time. The candidate was trained to many naturally distasteful practices, until humility made him fitted for full companionship with his brethren. Nothing super-fluous could belong to anyone of those monks, who thus voluntarily accepted a life of true poverty. Any person who really desired to follow this com-munity's rule was received, divested of all worldly goods, as if rescued from a shipwreck, with the loss of every article of his property. Nor would the holy superior, St. David, receive the smallest donation from a postulant as a contribution for the common support of their monastery. Such was the perfect spirit of abnegation, required by this most rigorous and ascetic rule.

Among all his spiritual children, St. David was most distinguished for his daily labours. He spent each day in teaching, in reading, in prayer, and in the government of his religious family. He also took care to provide for and feed orphans, widows, with other indigent persons. His heart glowed like a furnace of divine love, especially when he offered the holy sacrifice of the Lord's body and blood. He often poured forth floods of penitential tears. Engaged in meditation, he seemed to be holding conversation alone with the Angels of God. One of his penitential exercises consisted in the nightly and lengthened immersion of his body in cold water, so that he might perfectly subdue every rebellious movement of the flesh. When the rest of his monks sought a much-needed repose in their beds, the holy David alone frequently kept vigil, and offered his prayers to Almighty God, on behalf of that flock entrusted to his charge.*

St. David is said† to have been set up as a most eminent mirror and exemplar for all. His subjects were instructed by example, not less than by word. Although a great preacher, he was still greater in practical work. He conveyed instruction to his hearers, order to his religious, life to the destitute, support to the orphan, comfort to widows; he became the father of his scholars, a rule for his monks, and a guide for secular persons. Thus, he became all things to all men, that he might gain all to Christ.

---

* See, *Colgan's Acta Sanctorum Hiberniæ. 1 Martii. Vita S. Davidis.* §§ xii. xiii., pp. 426, 427. John Capgrave has nearly the same account, regarding our saint's mode of living. See, *Legenda Angliæ.*

† By Giraldus Cambrensis.

CHAPTER VII.

Many illustrious persons are attracted to St. David's rule of observance.—His miracles.—Various holy Irishmen become his
disciples—Ireland always regarded St. David with a special
veneration.

His fame then became so great, that by his means,
many kings and princes left the world and sought
cloistral shelter.　His monastery seemed the great
centre of religious attraction.　Among others, Constantine, king of Cornubia,* now Cornwall, abandon-
ing the early vices of his youth and all worldly
pleasures, took the habit of a monk in St. David's
monastery.　That he might become still more devoted
to the Almighty's service, he afterwards went over
to Ireland,† where he is said to have passed some
time, under the direction of St. Carthage, at Rathen,
near Tullamore.‡

Among many miracles recorded of our Saint, it
is said, that one day, whilst his brethren were assembled together, they complained that water was
wanting to them.　Their compassionate Father went

---

* Ricemarc calls him "rex," and Giraldus, "dux Cornubiæ."

† See, Hector Boetius, *Historia Scotorum.*　Lib. ix.

‡ The Acts of St. Constantine, King, Monk and Martyr are
given by Colgan, at the 11th of March, the date for his festival.
See, *Acta Sanctorum Hiberniæ,* pp. 577 to 579.

to a spot adjoining, where he held converse with an Angel. Here he prayed very fervently, asking the Almighty to supply what was necessary. Immediately a fountain of water issued from the earth. What seemed still more remarkable was a change of this water into wine, for the refreshment of St. David's monks.* This is related by Giraldus in a more diffuse and somewhat different manner. He tells us, the monks had desired, that a sufficient supply of clear running water should flow near the monastery, for sacramental celebration of the holy mysteries of our Lord's Body, offered at Mass. For a stream called Aluni, which ran through the valley, had often become turbid and discoloured, when it had not dried up in the summer season. Then their venerable superior went immediately to the cemetery, where he had Angelic conferences frequently; and for some time he prayed devoutly to our Lord. The clear fountain, which immediately issued from that spot, served for sacramental and general purposes, even to the time of Giraldus. Before his age, popular tradition had held, that this fountain sometimes flowed with wine; and it was a certain truth, says this writer, that milk issued from it, occasionally, so late as the twelfth century. Moreover, owing to the great merits of St. David and his monks, many

---

* See, Colgan's *Acta Sanctorum Hiberniæ.* 1 *Martii.* *Vita S. Davidis.* § xv. p. 427.

other fountains of water sprung up near the same place.*

In the Utrecht MS. it is related, that a rustic, called Tardus, said to St. David: "Our life is one of excessive toil, because our land lies far from the river, and we find the watering of it very laborious."† Wherefore, the holy David, having compassion on this peasant, drove the point of his staff into the earth. Suddenly, a clear fountain of cold water sprung up, and served to refresh the soil, during the heats of summer.‡

Whatever spiritual graces pious disciples receive, also reflect glory and honour on their holy masters. Many such worthy scholars flocked to the school of St. David ; and our Island furnished its fair contingent, as we read in the acts of our national saints. Aidan is repeatedly spoken of as St. David's disciple, not only in his own Life at the 31st of January,§ but likewise in David's Acts. From the former it

---

* *Vita S. Davidis. Lect.* v.

† "Ubi Breudi quoque, ubi ecclesia in honore Sancti David, quasi per milliaria quatuor a Meuevia distans, fundata dinoscitur, ad instantiam viri cujusdam, cui nomen Terdi, pulcherrimum dulcis aquæ fontem piis similiter supplicationibus pater emisit."—*Lect.* v. For "cui nomen Terdi," the Bollandists have "Quidam rusticus, nomine Tardi."—*Vita S. Davidis.* Cap. iii.

‡ See, *Acta Sanctorum Martii.* 1 *Martii. Vita S. Davidis.* Cap. iii. § 9, p. 43.

§ See, Colgan's *Acta Sanctorum Hiberniæ* at this day.

would appear, that Aidan was already grown when
he went to study under the Bishop of Menevia.*
Ussher was greatly puzzled by these authorities,
some of which are quoted by him.† He vainly endeavours to invalidate them ; *first*, by suggesting
that king Ainmire, with whom Aidan was kept as a
hostage, perhaps had been an older one bearing that
name ; and *secondly*, by observing, that what is said
regarding Aidan having been with St. David, may
be understood of that holy Irishman having studied
in David's monastery after the bishop of Menevia's
death.‡ The former evasion is indeed truly pitiful.
Where in the sixth century could a king over all
Ireland be found, who was called Ainmire, and different from him, who began to reign in 564 ? Besides,
Ussher knew very well, that Aidan flourished in the
latter end of the sixth century, and during no small
part of the seventh. This latter explanation cannot
be reconciled with passages found in the Lives of
our saints. Those are too numerous and too clear,
to be set aside, in this off-hand manner. We find

---

* In the Life of St. David by Giraldus, St. Aidan is said to
have been "divinis eruditus disciplinis," when under the tuition
of the saintly bishop of Menevia. "Quodam igitur die tres fidelis-
simi discipuli David ad ipsum veniunt; Aidanus scilicet, qui et
Hybernice *Maidaucus*; Eliud, qui et hodie *Teliau* dicitur; et
Ysmael."—*Lect.* iv.

† *Primordia*, p. 965.

‡ See, *Index Chronologicus*, A.D. DLXVI.

St. David introduced several times as speaking to or concerning Aidan, when in his monastery. In the Life of St. David,* we read that Aidan, after returning to Ireland, had sent a person to David, for the special purpose of guarding him from an attempt to take away his life, by poisoning some bread, which had been offered to him. This he blessed, when it divided into three portions, and without any hesitation, he eat one of these fragments, that contained no poison.

We are told, that a portion of Scripture had been transcribed by Maidoc. This was the Gospel of St. John, and he found an unfinished column on his return completed by an angel, in letters of gold. Through reverence for this *Codex*, it was long kept as a sealed book. Having been enclosed in cover, ornamented with gold and silver, no human eye had been permitted to inspect it, or to open the clasp. In the time of Giraldus, when the love and fear of God grew weak, and when the fervour of faith declined, some persons felt curious enough to examine this remarkable work. But, having had some internal monition, which taught them to dread a perilous result, they desisted from such rash experiment.†

---

* *Vita S. Davidis.*   Cap. xvii.

† Giraldus adds respecting this book : " Vocatur autem a comprovincialibus textus iste *Evangelium Imperfectum ;* qui usque in hodiernum signis clarus et virtutibus, in maxima non immerito

The Bollandists say, however, that in any Acts of St. David, which they had seen, no mention had been made regarding this work, written in golden characters, and completed by Angels. Such a remark has been incidentally made, when citing the testimony of Herman Greuen's additions to Usuard's Martyrology, where the foregoing account had been given.

A wood in which St. Maidoc wrought, was situated in a valley, known as Saleunach, about two miles distant from St. David's monastery.* His course of instruction caused the disciple to emulate his master's noble example. It is said, by Giraldus, that when Maidoc built a magnificent monastery at Ferns,† he called his own disciples together, and proposed to them the adoption of St. David's religious rule, which he studied at Menevia. This recommendation was adopted.

Another Irish disciple of St. David, called Scuthinus by Colgan and the Bollandists, is designated by Giraldus, Swithinus, or Scolanus, who was said to have been appointed bishop of Winton. Ricemarc calls him Scutinus; but he is silent, regarding the episcopacy of Winton having been conferred upon

---

reverentia a cunctis habetur.—*Lect.* vi. Ricemarc does not mention anything regarding this Codex.

* See Giraldus Cambrensis' account.

† Giraldus calls his place " Fernas," and Ricemarc " Guerwin."

him. This report, which Giraldus gives as such, cannot have been well founded ; for it appears referable to St. Swithun, who became bishop, A.D. 936, and who is venerated at the 2nd of July.

Speaking of that Scuthinus, who is venerated at the 2nd of January, in our Irish calendars, Giraldus Cambrensis, in his Life of St. David, has observed, that he was otherwise called Scolanus, after his promotion to the see of Winton. But, says the Bollandist editor, this seems to be St. Swithun, venerated on the 2nd of July, and who was successor of Helmstan, A.D. 936, as Wigorn relates in his chronicle.

Besides the foregoing holy Irishmen, we read of St. Barr or Barrocus having visited St. David, on returning from Rome. In giving us an account, of St. Barrock* meeting St. Brendan on the sea, Giraldus prefaces his observations with a remark, that in those times, it was a usual custom of the Irish, to make pious and laborious pilgrimages towards that holy city, in preference to any other place.† A strange legend is introduced, in connexion with this narrative.‡ We must remark, however, this account about St. Barr is altogether omitted from the Utrecht

---

* St. Barrocus is called Barre, by Ricemarc.

† See, *Lect.* vi.

‡ Giraldus concludes his account about Barr's return to Cork, by saying, that this saint related to the brethren what had occurred, and that these monks kept the horse on which he had been borne for their monastic purposes, to the day of his death. He

MS. The Bollandist editor attaches little importance to it; for he regards the story about St. Barr
of Cork visiting St. David, to be irreconcilable with
correct chronology. Being represented, as a disciple
of St. Gregory and returning from Rome; it is
thought, St. Barr could not have found St. David
then living. This account and that referring to St.
Swithin are supposed to have been merely poetic fig-
ments.* Modomnoc or Dominic,† the bee-keeper of

---

adds: " Post obitum vero ad tanti [et] tam inauditi miraculi per-
petuam memoriam, equum fusilem modicum et portabilem, virum-
que insidentem, auro et argento egregie distinctum fecerunt. Qui
usque in hodiernum Corcagiæ in ecclesia Barroci, signis clarus et
virtutibus, in maxima nimirum reverentia a comprovincialibus
haberi solet. His autem vehiculorum miraculis illud in Psalmo
consonare potest. " In mari via tua, et semita tua in aquis multis ;
et vestigia tua non cognoscentur." Item et illud in cantico Abba-
cuk: " Viam fecisti in mari equis tuis, in luto aquarum multarum."
Mirabilis itaque Deus in sanctis suis, et magnus in omnibus operi-
bus suis. Nec detestari debet, sed admirari, sed venerari, Crea-
toris opera, quævis creatura. " Multa nimirum" ut ait Jeronimus
" incredibilia reperies nec verisimilia, quæ nihilominus tamen vera
sunt." Nihil enim contra naturæ Dominum prævalet natura."
Lect. vi.

* The modern editor of Giraldus Cambrensis' works says :
" This legend is also found in the older life, published by the Bollandists, but is rejected by them as a later insertion. It is found
in all the early hagiologies, and is so completely Irish in its character, that its genuineness can hardly be disputed. No one would
now think of paring down these accounts to the dead level of historic prose."

† Giraldus calls Modomnoc, " Mandabaaucus." In the Utrecht
MS. we read *Modnuciant*, for Colgan's *Modomnoc*.

5

St. David, was an Irishman, who, after remaining
some time with his devout director, returned to his
own country. This monk is said to have been the
first person, who introduced bees into Ireland.*

Various reasons have been assigned by our
national hagiologist, Colgan, for placing St. David
of Wales, among the saints of Ireland. In the first
place, this patriarch's mother, by race, and family,
perhaps even by birth, had been Irish.† Secondly,
an affectionate and unalterable intimacy existed
between St. David, and some of the most eminent of our Irish saints, who either lived with
him for a time, as disciples and scholars, or who
claimed his friendship and religious services.
Thirdly, by our national hagiologists and martyrologists, we find his name and festival set down in
native calendars and martyrologies, with the saints

---

* Ricemarc says: " In Hibernia nunquam ad illud tempus apes
vivere poterant. Nam si Hiberniensem humum aut lapidem mediis
apibus immitteres; dispersæ atque fugaces nimium devitarent."
Giraldus attributes this importation of most useful insects, to St.
Dominick of Ossory, on the assertion of some writers. See, *Topo-
graphia Hibernica. Distinctio* 1. *Cap.* vi. *Opera, vol.* v.

† Her father Bracan was son to Halulph, an Irish King or Prince.
See, Albertus le Grande, *De Sanctis Armoricæ. Vita S. Cadoci,*
1 *Novembris.* And William Camden in his account of Great Britain, notes to *Itinerarium Cambriæ,* Lib. i. Cap. ii. In the Acts,
and notes thereto, of St. Canoc, at the 11th of February, Colgan,
likewise, treats on this subject.

of our own country. This is quite an unusual distinction, when a saint had not been known, as connected with Ireland, by birth, residence, or death.* Fourthly, among the Acts of Irish saints, found in the *Codex Kilkenniensis* and Book of the Island, those of St. David, Bishop of Menevia, are included. To the foregoing, we may be permitted to append an observation, that the name, festival, patronage and memory of St. David, for a long period have been held in veneration, by the inhabitants of our own Green Island; and in various localities there, churches and religious houses have cherished his patronage and protection.

---

* St. Ænguss and the Martyrology of Tallagh, Marianus Gorman, Maguire and the Martyrology of Donegall, have notices of St. David, at the date assigned for his festival.

CHAPTER VIII.

St. David, with St. Eliud and St. Paterone, visits Jerusalem.—
The gift of tongues.—Hospitably received by the Patriarch.—
St. David's consecration.—Preaching of those holy missionaries,
and numbers of people conve.ted.—Presents received on their
return to Britain.—The Pelagian heresy—Synod convoked at
Brevi.—A great multitude assembled there, to whom St. David
preaches.—Miraculous manifestations—He is created Archbishop
over the Britons.

St. David was commanded by an angel to repair to
Jerusalem with two of his companions, named Eliud
or Teilo, and Padarn or Paterone.* He asked the
Angel, how this matter could be accomplished, as
both of those holy men were then living far apart
from him, and from each other. The Angel then
said, he would bring all three together, and that they
should meet at an appointed place. All matters
being thus arranged, St. David repaired towards the

* " *Patern*, of a noble family in *Armorica*, having studied 20
years in *Ireland*, came and settled in *Cambria*, where he usefully
employed his time in promoting peace among the several Princes.
He generally resided at Cardigan, where is still to be seen *Llan-
Badarn-vawr*, that is, *The Church of great St. Patern*, which for
some time was a Bishop's seat.. *Patern* died in his native country,
where he was so distinguished for holiness of life, that no less
than three Festival-days were dedicated to his Memory."—Rapin's
History of England. Vol. i. book ii. p. 43.

sea-shore. As the Angel had promised, both of his designated companions joined him. They formed one band, and all were regarded as on an equal footing. Accordingly he and his two companions set out, with one heart and will. But, on reaching France, and hearing its people speak in a different language from that of their own native land; God bestowed on David and his friends the gift of tongues, so that, during the whole of their journey, they did not need an interpreter.* They were even found capable of speaking strange dialects. Furthermore, the Almighty was pleased to direct their course towards Jerusalem. But, before they had entered this renowned and hallowed city, the Angel of God visited its Patriarch† in a dream. This

---

* We are informed, there was a great similarity in the lives and actions of Dewi, Padarn and Teilo, and that, on such account, they are frequently joined together in the Welsh Triads. They are called the three Blessed Visitors and the three Blessed Bards of the Isle of Britain. David is said to have performed Divine Service, in a more pleasing manner, than either of his companions; Padarn sang in a superior style; and Teilo surpassed either of the former, as an excellent preacher. See, Rev. John Williams' *Ecclesiastical Antiquities of the Cymry.* Chap. v. p. 133.

† The Patriarch of Jerusalem, at this time, was John III., as the Bollandists prove, in the Life of S. Theodosius the Cœnobiarch, published at the 11th of January. See these notices of Theodosius in *Acta Sanctorum Januarii. Tomus* 1. xi. *Januarii. Vita S. Theodosii,* pp. 680 to 701. The Bollandists assign this visit of St. David, and his consecration at Jerusalem, to about A.D. 516, or almost immediately after this year.

Angel said to him : " Three Catholics from the bounds of the West are coming to thee. Receive them with honour. One of these, named David, you shall consecrate Archbishop." The Patriarch greatly rejoiced, on hearing these words, and afterwards he received the holy strangers with marked distinction.

On reaching Jerusalem, they were graciously and hospitably entertained by the Patriarch.* David himself, as we are told, was consecrated Archbishop. All three were commanded by this Patriarch to preach to the Jews, and to other heretical opponents of the Catholic Church. They were exhorted to regard this office as their special duty, being true

---

* The Irish custom of making pilgrimages to Rome, at this period and subsequently, is mentioned by Ricemarc, in his life of St. David, " cum inextinguibile Hibernensium desiderium ad sanctorum Petri e: Pauli apostolorum reliquias visitandas arderet." See, Dr. Moran's valuable and learned *Essays on the Origin, Doctrines, and Discipline of the Early Irish Church.* Part iii. chap. iii. p. 150. On this particular subject, there are multiplied instances and proofs, afforded by the author, regarding Irish Pilgrimages made to Rome, from the days of St. Patrick to periods long subsequent. We have no mention about St. David having visited Rome ; yet, it is possible, he may have journeyed thither, on his going to or returning from Jerusalem. However, as he does not at first appear to have been consecrated bishop, or as Rome might have taken him too far away from a direct course, or as want of time, opportunity, means, &c., might not have permitted, St. David may have been obliged to forego his wishes, on this matter of accomplishing a Roman pilgrimage.

soldiers of Christ, wielding the buckler of Faith and the sword of the Spirit, which is the word of God. They were required to preach the Scriptures daily, that so they might frustrate and overcome their spiritual adversaries.* These commands were duly obeyed, and the Gospel was announced every day. Their labours were crowned with a fruitful harvest of souls. Many were brought into the fold of Christ's Church. Many believers also were still more confirmed in the Faith.

This happy and fruitful pilgrimage had brought with it a term, when the Almighty wished his faithful servants' return towards their own country. As parting gifts, the Patriarch bestowed on blessed David four different objects. These were intended to serve for religious *souvenirs* of the time spent by him in a land so celebrated, and which had been the immediate scene of so many great mysteries and miracles effected when our Lord Jesus appeared to men upon earth. They were a consecrated portable altar,†

---

* Giraldus says, that at this time the fury of the Gentiles—Ricemarc says of the Jews—greatly prevailed against the Christians. The Patriarch obtained the consent of our saints, to spread the Gospel "in Oriéntis aliquamdiu partibus," &c.—*Lect.* vii

† "In quo Dominicum sacrabat corpus," adds the Utrecht MS., "quod innumeris virtutibus pollens, nunquam ab hominibu ab ejus Pontificis obitu visum est: sed pelleis velaminibus tectum absconditum latet insigni etiam nola: sed et ipsa virtutibus claret: baculo et tunica ex auro texta."

a staff, a bell,* and a tunic;† These presents
were held in the greatest veneration, as relics, and

---

* We learn from Ranulph Higden's *Polychronicon*, that in
Wales, as in Ireland and Scotland, bells and crooked staves,
(croziers) were held in great veneration, and people feared to
commit perjury, when swearing on them.

> " In hac quoque provincia,
> Hibernia, et Scotia
> Campanæ sunt et baculi
> Ornata sub multiplici,
> Tam digni procul dubio
> In clero et in populo,
> Quod vereantur hodie
> Perjurium committere
> Tam super horum alterum,
> Quam super evangelium."

(Vol. i. Lib. i. pp. 426, 428.)

See the edition, edited by Churchill Babington, B.D., and published under direction of the Master of the Rolls.

† In the Life of St. Telius, says the Bollandist editor, it is
related, the bell was his peculiar gift, and that St. Padarn received
a "baculus" and "cappa choralis." In Capgrave's *Vita S. Patricii* we read, " S. David lapidem, quem a Patriarcha Hierosoly-
mitano in sua consecratione acceperat, adhuc vivens Ecclesiæ
Glastoniensi delegavit." The Patriarch, in the Utrecht MS., is
said to have told these saints, to return in peace towards their
own country, and that these gifts should afterwards reach them.
The guardian Angel of each is said to have brought his own gift
to every one of those saints, when he had arrived at his own
religious house. David was then found at his monastery, named
Langemelech—by Giraldus it is called Langevelach. " Inde ea
vocat vulgus cœlo venientia," adds the Utrecht MS. Giraldus
says, the bell and altar were regarded as instrumental in working
miracles at his day; and that the gifts of Paternus and Eliud,
preserved in their monasteries, were similarly signalized.

were long afterwards preserved. Through them, many miracles are said to have been wrought, in various places.*

Either before or after his consecration, David founded a monastery in the Valley of Rosina,† which¹ was afterwards called Menevia. Here he lived in seclusion, for some time, till he was called to the synod of Brefi.‡ Amidst many calamities that befel their country, the Britons found themselves involved in theological disputes. About the commencement of the fifth century, these controversies led to what

---

* See, *Colgan's Acta Sanctorum Hiberniæ.* 1 *Martii. Vita S. Davidis* §§ xx. xxi. xxii. p. 428.

† Sometimes called Ross, Rosnaut or Rosnat. It was situated in Pembrokeshire. Frequent mention is made regarding this monastery, in the acts of various Irish saints. It was reputed as one of their foreign colleges.

‡ This Synod of Brevy—confounded by Colgau (note 27) with the " Synod of Victory"—is said to have assembled, A.D. 519. See, Bale, *Century* i. cap. 55, and Ussher's *Britannicarum Ecclesiarum Antiquitates Index Chronologicus.* A.D. DXIX. p. 526. Endeavouring to account for the large number of bishops here assembled, Colgan observes, formerly in the British and Irish Church, Bishops were much more numerous than at a later period. He says, there were many titular bishops, who had no determinate dioceses or subjects. St. Patrick is said to have consecrated 350 bishops, under his own hand; but it does not follow, that all these held different sees, " nisi nomine sedium intelligamus ipsa Monasteria, quorum prelati passim creabantur Episcopi."—*Acta Sanctorum Hiberniæ.* 1 *Martii. Vita S. Davidis,* n. 27, p. 432.

has been since called the Pelagian heresy. This
appellation it derived from Pelagius, a Briton, who
broached heterodox and dangerous errors, regarding
the nature of Divine Grace and Original Sin. In
advancing such opinions, he was sustained by Celes-
tius, a Scot, and a disciple, named Agricola. The
British Bishops sought the assistance of their Gallic
brethren, to refute the subtleties of these heresiarchs.
Having obtained permission from Pope Celestine I.,
St. Germanus, Bishop of Auxerre, visited Britain,
on two different occasions. In 429 he came, accompanied by St. Lupus, Bishop of Troyes, and again
in 446, with Severus of Treves.* The opinions of
Pelagius were finally condemned and suppressed,
whilst judicious efforts were made to counteract
them. Schools and seminaries for clerical education
supplied at length a much needed requirement in
various dioceses.†

---

* Both St. Germanus and St. Lupus, in a conference with the
Pelagians at Verulam, defended the truth with such constancy
and evidence, that many turned from former errors. " But after
their departure, the *Hereticks* gaining ground again, Germanus
was desired once more to come over. Though he was now very
old, he undertook a second voyage into *Britain*, in company with
Severus, Bishop of *Troye*." See, Rapin de Thoyras' *History of
England, Translated by N. Tindal, M.A.* Vol. i. Book i. p. 29.
London: 1743, folio. Third Edition.

† See, *Dr. Lingard's History of England.* Vol. i. chap. i. A.D.
449, p. 58.

At that time, when the Pelagian heresy was again growing rife in Britain, a numerous Synod of Bishops was summoned. So great was the throng of people, that they crowded all the surrounding neighbourhood, when this convocation took place. They assembled at a place called Brevi, and hence it is known as the Synod of Brevy.* One account has it, that no less than one hundred and eighteen bishops† were present, together with an almost limitless gathering of Abbots, Religious, Clerics, Kings, Princes and Nobles.‡ This multitudinous gathering resembled in some measure one of those great " monster meetings," with which the passing generation of our own countrymen must

---

* In "Ceretica regione"—now Cardiganshire—according to Giraldus Cambrensis. See *Vita S. Davidis*. This place is also called Llan-Deuy Breuy, which is Latinized, "templum S. Davidis Breuiense."' It may be Anglicised as *the church of St. David near the River Brevi*. See, also, *Itinerarium Cambria*. Lib. ii. cap. 4.

† Capgrave and Giraldus Cambrensis do not mention the number of bishops present. The latter, however, calls this " universali totius Kambriæ Synodo."

‡ In Wilkins' *Concilia Magnæ Britanniæ et Hiberniæ*, vol. i. p. 8, there is a brief account of what is called *Synodus Menevensis*, which is identified with the Synod of Brevi. Its chronology has been thus determined : " Papæ Rom. Hormisd. 6. Anno Christi 519. Imperat. Justin. sen. 2." It is said to have been convened under St. David, "contra fecem Palagianæ hœresis adhuc redolentem." The account, given by Wilkins, is chiefly extracted from Balaeus, Centur. i. cap. 55, and from the Eighth Lesson of St. David's Life, by Cambrensis.

be tolerably familiar ; for we are told, that a trumpet, much less a human voice, could hardly be expected to sound in the ears of all present. It was feared, that if this great multitude could not hear a preacher, the leaven of heresy must remain amongst them.*

This great Synod had assembled within Cardiganshire. A discussion then arose among the Bishops, as to who should preach to so great a multitude.† It was determined, at last, that he who could preach, so as to be heard by all, should be named Metropolitan. A heap of garments was piled together, and this served as an open-air tribune. Bishop after Bishop arose. But their voices could scarcely be heard by their next neighbours, for a great tumult arose among the people. The ecclesiastics especially felt some degree of trepidation, lest the crowd might continue irresolute or unconvinced regarding the true nature of those subtle controversies discussed or treated on in this large assembly. The clerics regarded their labour as already lost, until one of the Bishops, named Pauli-

---

* Of the people, Giraldus says, " hæretica pravitate pene irrevocabiliter infectum, ad fidei reducere tramitem non prævaluisset."—*Vita S. Davidis.*

† According to an account of this Synod, we are said to possess only the names of " Dyvrig, Pawl Hen, Deiniol, Dewi, Cattwg and Cybi."—Rev. John Williams' *Ecclesiastical Antiquities of the Cymry.* Chap. xiv. p. 237, note. This writer assigns the usual date, A.D. 519, for the Synod of Brevi.

nus, with whom David formerly studied, rising in their midst, said before all: "There is indeed a Bishop here, who has been consecrated by the Patriarch of Jerusalem; he is eloquent, has a beautiful countenance, is filled with the grace of God, and of approved height* and figure, for the Angel of the Lord is his companion. Therefore, call him to your council." Having heard these words, messengers were sent to invite St. David's attendance. Such, however, had been his humble and retiring nature,† that three different times he wished to decline their invitation. At last, two venerable men, St. Daniel and St. Dubritius,‡ were sent to him. Owing to their persuasions, he consented to come.

---

* "Quatuor cubitorum statura erectus," adds the Utrecht MS.

† "Erat enim vir sanctus, contemplationi deditus : de temporalibus rebus et secularibus, nisi necessitate urgentiore compulsus, aut nihil aut parum curans."—Giraldus Cambrensis, *Vita S. Davidis.*

‡ "Dubricius died in the Isle of *Bardsey* in 522," according to Rapin. See, *History of England.* Vol. i. book ii. (note (1), p. 43. Translation by N. Tindal, M.A. His demise took place on the 14th of November. St. Daniel was the first bishop of Bangor, near Anglesea, about A.D. 516, or perhaps later. He was consecrated by his master St. Dubritius, bishop, or as sometimes called archbishop of Landaff, or Legionensis, as we are told, by the Bollandist editor. St. Daniel's feast occurs on the 1st of December, according to the English Martyrology, and that of St. Dubritius on the 14th of November, with his translation at the 8th of May. The Martyrology of Tallaght, Marianus and Maguire, place St. Daniel's festival at the 11th of September. See, Rev. Dr. Kelly's *Martyro-*

On his way to the Synod, it is related, that a woman placed the dead body of her son* before St. David. She besought him in tears, to bring her offspring once again to life. The compassionate Bishop, touched by her misfortune, offered his prayers to God, when the boy was soon restored to life and health. Transported with joy, his mother cried out; "My son that had died, through God's favour and yours, now lives!" The holy Bishop David then lifting this boy in his arms, placed him on his own shoulders, and thus conveyed him towards the Synod. This child afterwards ended his days by a holy death.

When St. David arrived, all those constituting the Synod, especially the secular and regular clergy, greatly rejoiced. Being asked to preach, he humbly consented. On rising for this purpose, in presence of a vast multitude, a snow-white dove seemed coming down from Heaven, and at length, it alighted on the shoulders of St. David.† With clear intonation,

---

logy of Tallagh, p. xxxiv. It is supposed, he was thus ranked with the Irish Saints, because he lived an eremitical life, for some years, at Inis-angin, in Lough Ree, as would appear from a Life of St. Kieran of Clonmacnois (*Cap.* 25). He is supposed to have died, between the years 542 and 545.

* " Cui barbara imperitia Magnum nomen dederat," adds the Utrecht MS.

† Colgan remarks, that the descent of a snow-white dove is a circumstance often noted in the Acts of various saints. Thus, at

and as if with trumpet notes, he begun to announce
the word of God.* He met all objections advanced
for the prevailing heresy, and admirably refuted
them, whilst he proved most convincingly the tenets
of Holy Church. He gained all hearts by his eloquent and persuasive words, so that the entire multitude gave thanks to the Almighty and to our
Saint. Meantime, the earth appeared to swell
beneath his feet, until the preacher, ascending above
the crowd, was distinctly seen by all present, as if
standing upon a high hill.†

He preached in so loud, and full a voice, that he
was heard by all present; by those who were near,
as well as by those, who were obliged to remain afar.
With consent of all Prelates, Kings and Chieftains

---

the ordination of St. Sampson, as Capgrave relates in his Life of
St. Dubricius; likewise, at the ordination of St. Fabian Pope, as
stated by Eusebius, *Lib.* 6, *cap.* 22, and by Baronius, at A.D. 238.
Again, in the case of St. Papeus, as related in the Acts of St.
Endeus of Arran, at the 21st of March. See, *Acta Sanctorum
Hiberniæ.* 1 *Martii. Vita S. Davidis,* n. 29, p. 432, and *Ibid.*
xxi. *Martii. Vita S. Endei.* Cap. xix. p. 708.

* "Juxta illud: 'Aperi os tuum, et ego adimplebo illud.' Et
alibi: 'Cum steteritis ante reges et præsides, nolite cogitare, quo-
modo aut quid loquamini. Dabitur enim vobis illa hora quid
loquamini.' Et subsequenter: 'Non enim vos estis, qui loquamini,
sed Spiritus Patris vestri, qui loquitur in vobis.' "— *Giraldus Cambrensis' Vita S. Davidis, Lect.* viii.

† On the top of this hill a church stood, at the time the author
of the Utrecht MS. wrote.

there, he was named Archbishop of Britain.* To this arrangement he reluctantly assented. The city, in which he was destined to reside, had been raised to the dignity of a Metropolitical see.† The date of St. David's elevation to the episcopal dignity has been left very much an open question, for chronographers to determine.‡ That St. David belonged wholly to the sixth century, is Dr. Lanigan's opinion, he being contemporary with Irish saints of the second order. As for certain biographical writers, who made him a bishop in the fifth century, they are not worth attending to, in the estimation of this learned Doctor.

It hardly falls within our province to treat on the origin of Menevia; or rather a removal thither of old Caer-leon see, in the time of David's incumbency, as

---

* Giraldus says: "Pater autem David communi omnium tam cleri scilicet quam populi, electione pariter et acclamatione, cui et honorem antea destinatione Dubricius cesserat, in Kambriæ totius archiepiscopum est sublimatus." *Lect.* viii.

† The account adds: "Ita ut quicumque in ea præsideret in posterum Archipræsul haberetur." See, Colgan's *Acta Sanctorum Hiberniæ.* 1 *Martii. Vita S. Davidis.* § xxiii. pp. 428, 429.

‡ Colgan tells us, that Radulphus de Baldock, Bishop of London, in his Chronicle, and a certain anonymous chronicler, belonging to the Church of Menevia, have assigned his accession to A.D. 561. See, *Acta Sanctorum Hiberniæ.* 1 *Martii. Vita S. Davidis,* n. 31, p. 432. Yet, the Bollandists think, St. David immediately succeeded as Archbishop, after the death of Dubritius, A.D. 522.

ratified by the famous synod of Brevy.* Caer-leon was then a populous city, whilst Menevia, remotely situated, seemed destined only for solitude, being almost separated from other parts of Britain.†

Certain rather modern writers would make St. David a bishop before A.D. 519,‡ remarks Dr. Lani-

---

* These points have been illustrated with much accuracy, both by Ussher, in his *Britannicarum Ecclesiarum Antiquitates*, as also by Stillingfleet in his *Antiquities of the British Churches*. At the church of Llan Devi Brevi, a curious inscription was found by Mr. Lluyd, on a stone set over the chancel door. The inhabitants said this commemorated a person struck dead by St. David, for letting loose a mischievous beaver, after it had been ensnared with difficulty. This inscription is preserved. The sexton of the church showed him a rarity called, *Matkorn yr ych bannog*, or *Matkorn ych Dewi*, which was said to have been there preserved from the time of St. David. He added the fable of the oxen called *Ychen bannog*, which drew away a monstrous beaver dead. "If this Matkorn is not the interior part of an ox's horn as its name imports, it very much resembles it, and is so heavy that it seems absolutely petrified." Gough's Camden's *Britannia*, vol. ii. p. 527.

† Ralph of Chester in his Chronicle, *Lib*. i. *cap*. 52, states, that by favour of King Arthur, St. David had been allowed to transfer the seat of episcopacy from Caer-leon to Menevia.

‡ Ussher follows Bale, in his *Index Chronologicus*, and places this synod at A.D. 519. In an addition to Camden (*col.* 768), Gibson says it was held about 522. Whilst treating of it, Wilkins does not venture to decide on the time, when this synod was held. See, *Concilia Magnæ Britanniæ*. Tom. i. p. 7. "*Llandewi brewi*," says Leland, "is but a simple or poor village set among mountains every way but the west, where is the vale of Tyve. I

6

gan, as this year is assigned for holding the synod
of Brevy, in which our saint acted so conspicuous a
part, and when the see of Menevia is said to have
been declared metropolitical. But there is still
better authority for supposing, observes this same
writer, that he did not become bishop until about
540,* a date, which it is thought agrees with accounts
appearing most worthy of credit. But such a date
cannot be made to harmonize with Ussher's hypothesis, which many other writers have followed, of
St. David having died in or about A.D. 544.† It

---

passed over a little brook to enter into it. The collegiate church
of prebendaries standeth somewhat upon a high ground, but it is
rude." Vol. v. p. 75. This was founded in honour of St. David,
for a precentor and twelve prebends by Thomas Bek, bishop of St.
David's, A.D. 1187. See, Tanner's *Notitia Monastica*, p. 77.

* Considerable diversity of opinion appears to have existed on
this point. Ranulph of Chester, who is quoted by Ussher (p. 82),
says, that David was made bishop of Menevia, the very year, when
Pope Silverius died, *i.e.* A.D. 540. In Gale's edition of Ranulph
(xv. *Scriptores*), we do not find mention made of St. David. Even
if proceeding from an interpolator, this note is of old standing.
The interpolator of Marianus Scotus has the year 543 marked for
David's promotion. Others have 565, owing to a mistake in not
understanding certain chronological terms. See, Le Neve's *Fasti
Ecclesiæ Anglicanæ*, p. 510. But this date is considered quite too
late, nor can it be reconciled with any very credible authority,
which records the acts of St. David.

† Believing David died about that period, Ussher preferred the
date 544 to A.D. 546, given by William of Malmesbury, or A.D.
547 preferred by others, because Giraldus Cambrensis intimates

seems pretty certain, that David governed the Menevian see for several years, although their precise
number cannot be ascertained with any great degree
of exactness.*

---

that David's death happened on a Tuesday. "Now, in the year
544, the 1st of March fell on Tuesday. This is a good argument
against any other year about that time, but not against our being
allowed to suppose that David died several years later than 544 ;
whereas the 1st of March fell also on Tuesday in the years 550,
561, 567, 578, 589, 595, 600, &c. Passing by Creasy and other
copyists of Ussher, the Bollandists, and the minor writers of Lives
of Saints, and even the author of *L'art de verifier les dates* (at
Chronologie des Saints), have adopted his computation, as if the
question had been decided."—Lanigan's *Ecclesiastical History of
Ireland*, vol. i. chap. ix. § ix. n. 142, p. 473.

* Godwin, *De præsulibus Angliæ, ad Episc. Menev.*, maintains
that his episcopacy continued for sixty-five years. If any foundation for this statement existed, it would overturn Ussher's hypothesis. According to Ussher, calculating from A.D. 462 to A.D.
544, St. David must have died at the age of eighty-two. Now if
he were a bishop for sixty-five years, he should have been consecrated, according to Dr. Lanigan's opinion, when only seventeen
years old. No one will admit this early age, as a time suitable
for assuming the responsibilities of such an office. See, *Ecclesiastical History of Ireland*, vol. i. chap. ix. § ix. and n. 143, pp.
470, 472, 473.

CHAPTER IX.

The probable succession of bishops in the see of Carleon.—The
"Synod of Victory" there assembled.—Its decrees and happy
results.—Removal of the see from Carleon to Menevia.—St.
Kentigern's visit to the holy Archbishop.

WHEN the Synod of Brevy had been held, say the
Bollandists, the Archiepiscopal See of Wales was
established in the city of Carleon, on the Usk, Osk
or Isk river. This city also obtained the name
Legio. We are told, that Gistilianus, an uncle of
St. David, had been a bishop of Carleon.* St.
Dubricius then presided over Carleon see, and that
of Landaff, having succeeded St. Teliaus, second
bishop over this latter diocese.† Some writers have
supposed, that St. Dubricius, leaving Landaff and
Carleon to St. Teliaus, had been transferred as
Archbishop to Menevia, which he again resigned to
St. David. The Bollandists consider it more probable, that having died A.D. 522, or having been
rendered through old age unable to discharge his
episcopal duties, Dubricius had left the church of

---

* See, Winkles's *Cathedral Churches of England and Wales.*
Vol. iii. p. 129.

† At the 9th of February, John Bollandus has learnedly exa-
mined intricacies regarding this period of early British History.

Landaff to be ruled over by Teliaus, and that of Carleon by David. It is supposed, our saint may have thence removed to Menevia, still retaining his Archiepiscopal rank and office ; or he may have become bishop of Menevia, while Dubricius yet lived. The latter having died, St. David possibly became Archbishop over Cambria, with the approval of his reputed uncle, King Arthur.*

Having thus successfully defended the cause of Catholic Truth, the dogmas of Faith were announced, authentic seals were attached to those decrees, and St. David was then named to the Archbishopric. As the Pelagian heresy was not entirely suppressed, St. David convened another synod of all the Cambrian clergy at Carleon,† which proved so successful that Pelagianism was' exterminated. This Synod was termed the " Synod of Victory."‡ Many necessary

---

* " *Hæc nos ibi conjectavimus,*" say the Bollandists, " *non auri fidere Actis S. Davidis, secundum quæ in Synodo Breviensi est* Archiepiscopus constitutus, cui eum honorem antea destinatione Dubricium cessisse."

† This Synod is thought to have been held, A.D. 529. Its canons are said to have been "lost by means of the frequent incursions of pirates on the coasts of Wales." See, Rev. John Williams's *Ecclesiastical Antiquities of the Cymry.* Chap. xiv. p. 237 and note *ib.* Also, Ussher's Chronological Index, at A.D. DXXIX., under which year it is placed. See, *Britannicarum Ecclesiarum Antiquitates,* p. 528.

‡ In Wilkin's *Concilia Magnæ Britanniæ et Hiberniæ,* vol. i. pp. 8, 9, we have only a very short account regarding " Synodus

and useful decrees were passed and afterwards signed
by the Sovereign Pontiff. He even prescribed the
observance of statues, framed at both of those Synods,
in the churches and monasteries of Britain. Here,
they served to form a rule and code of Christian
life, and they were written by the hand of our holy
Prelate. It is greatly to be regretted, that these
decrees have not survived the wreck of many other
ancient records.[*]

The good fruits resulting from both these Synods
soon became apparent. Churches and monasteries
increased in number and good government. Works
of charity and religion extended among the faithful.
The Holy David seemed like a ruler set by our Lord
over the house of Israel. In his learning, discipline
and life, he was a perfect example for his flock to
follow. With judgment and care, he provided for
all necessities of his people. Like a pious father
and revered shepherd, he assisted those subject to
him. It would be impossible to enumerate the many
virtues which exalted his character, or various ad-

Victoriæ in Wallia." This is taken from the Ninth Lesson of St
David's Life, by Cambrensis. The editor prefixes " anno incerto,"
to this notice.

[*] Giraldus says of them: " Quæ quidem, sicut et alii quam
plurimi nobilis bibliothecæ thesauri egregii, tam vetustate quam
incuria, piratarum quoque crebris insultibus, qui de Orcadum insulis
æstivo tempore longis navibus advecti maritimas Kambriæ pro-
vincias vastare consueverant, evanuerunt."—*Lect.* ix.

vantages procured for his ecclesiastical charge. And in the discharge of those religious duties, his life is said to have reached an extraordinary term of duration.*

As Archbishop he first resided at Carleon upon Usk ;† but he soon obtained permission from King Arthur‡ to remove his see to Menevia, now St.

---

* See, Colgan's *Acta Sanctorum Hiberniæ.* 1 *Martii.* *Vita S. Davidis.* §§ xxiv. xxv. p. 429.

† To this place, we are told, as a metropolitical see, the British bishoprics were subject, for a long time. See, *Polychronicon.* Lib. i. cap. 52.

‡ " His nephew," according to Selden's *Illustrations* to Drayton's *Poly-Olbion.* *The Fourth Song.* From a translation of the Seventh Historical Triad, we learn, that the following three were enthroned Persons in the Isle of Britain : " Arthur as sovereign prince (yn benteyrned) in Caerlleon upon Usk, and Dewi (David) the head bishop, and Maelgon of Gwynez the chief elder (ben hynain); Arthur as sovereign prince at Celliwig in Cornwall, and Bedwini the head bishop, and Caradoc with the brawny arm (vreiçvras) the chief elder; Arthur as sovereign prince at the promontory of Rionyz in the north, and Cyndeyrn Garthwys (Kentigern) the head bishop, and Gwrthmwl Wledig the chief elder." See, Sharon Turner's *History of the Anglo-Saxons.* Vol. i. book ii. chap. v. pp. 250, 251. In this same chapter, the reader will find an interesting account about the renowned King Arthur and his achievements. His history will serve to recall, those noble lines of our Irish poet, Davis :—

" Then send out a thunder shout, and every true man summon,
   Till the ground shall echo round from Severn to Plinlimmon,
      ' Saxon foes and Cymric brothers,
         ' Arthur's come again !' "

Poems. *Cymric Rule and Cymric Rulers,* p. 43.

David's, in Pembrokeshire.* Such permission having
been obtained, the change of see was effected.† This
translation of the Archbishopric is said to have been
foretold by Merlin :‡ " Menevia shall put on the Pall
of Carleon ; and the preacher of Ireland shall wax
dumb by an infant growing in the womb."§

In the Life of St. Kentigern, Bishop of Glasgow,
it is said, that certain children of Belial, belonging
to King Morken's kindred, had conspired to effect
the death of this holy man. Whereupon, having had
a Divine admonition, he directed his course towards
Menevia, where St. David had already acquired a
great reputation, owing to his distinguished virtues.
Near Carleum‖ St. Kentigern converted many to the

---

* "Cambriæ Metropolites et Primas propterea factus, tantam
cum Rege Arthuro gratiam iniit, ut ab urbe Legionum ad suam
Mcneviam Archiepiscopalem transferret sedem, ut lib. i. cap. 52
fusius tradit Ranulfus Cestriensis." Spelman's *Concilia, Decreta,
Leges, Constitutiones in Re Ecclesiarum Orbis Britannici*, p. 62.

† This is certified by Giraldus Cambrensis in *Itinerarium Cambriæ*. Lib. ii. cap. 4, and Ralph of Chester in *Polychronicon*. Lib.
i. cap. 52.

‡ For authority, *Alan. de Insul.* i. *ad Prophet. Merlini*, is
quoted.

§ " This was performed, " we are told, " when St. Patrick, at
presence of Melaria then with child, suddenly lost use of his
speech ; but recovering it after some time, made prediction of
Dewy's holiness, joined with greatness, which is so celebrated.
Upon my author's credit only believe me." See, Selden's *Illustrations to Drayton's Poly-Olbion. The Fifth Song.*

‖ Carleon ?

faith and built a church. He remained some short time with our saint. This journey is assigned to A.D. 543,* by Ussher. It is said, he obtained a place for building a monastery from Cathwal, a king in this part of the country. Again, we find it related, that he composed a very elegant and erudite discourse on the death of St. David, besides leaving other learned works behind him.† These, however, the Bollandists considered to have been lost.‡

---

* The Bollaudists, regarding this as the last year before David's death, think St. Kentigern might have procured many accounts through our saint's own narrative. From such materials, perhaps, he might have written that obituary discourse attributed to him, after the death of the holy Menevian bishop.

† Pitseus, Bale, and Leland are cited, as authorities for statements in the text.

‡ See, *Acta Sanctorum Martii. Tomus* i. *Martii* 1. *Vita S. Davidis. Commentarius Prævius.* § i. n. 6, p. 39. They have published St. Kentigern's Acts, at the 13th of January. See, *Acta Sanctorum Januarii. Tomus* i. pp. 815 to 821.

CHAPTER X.

Our Saint receives a heavenly admonition regarding his death.—
His pious resignation to the Divine will.—A foreknowledge of
his decease conveyed to the people of Britain and Ireland.—
The last hours of St. David.—Discordant dates regarding the
year when he died.—His extraordinary longevity.—Opinions
of various writers.

At last, having attained the extraordinary age of
147 years, the Almighty deemed his days and vir-
tuous acts sufficiently ripe for Heavenly rest and
reward. He was admonished by an angel, about
his approaching death, on the viii. of the March
Kalends, corresponding with the 22nd of February.
His religious brethren had been engaged, reciting
the Lauds of their Holy Office, at an early morning
hour, when this Angelic voice was heard : " Behold,
David, the day thou hast desired approaches !" The
venerable bishop heard this summons with delight.
In a transport of joy, he cried out : " Now, O Lord,
dismiss thy servant in peace !"* The monks, who
were present, heard this miraculous colloquy ; but
not fully understanding its import, they fell prostrate
on earth. The venerable bishop, standing with his
countenance and thoughts alike raised towards Hea-

---

* See, *Luke* ii. 29.

ven, exclaimed : "O Lord, receive my spirit!" In
the hearing of his monks, the Angel again replied :
".Prepare thyself for the Kalends of March, for then
Jesus Christ, the King of this world, shall meet
thee, and with him will be many thousands of
Angels." Sadness filled the hearts of his spiritual
children, when they heard this announcement. But
the blessed David consoled them, saying : "My
brethren, persevere, and bear to the end, that yoke
you have received." Soon were sorrow and lamen-
tations diffused throughout his favoured city. Tears
and pious impetrations were poured out by all its
inhabitants. And as the Angelic words sounded in
his ears, a most enchanting concert of Angelic choirs
was heard, while a fragrance, surpassing earth's
most odoriferous perfumes, was wafted throughout
the city of Menevia.

How delightfully instructive are the examples left
to Christians by God's saints, especially during those
days, when life fast draws towards its closing scenes.
Some Angelic monition regarding such events appears to have spread a rumour, not alone through
all Britain, but even throughout the whole of Hibernia. The holy men of both Islands assembled
together, like flocks of birds flying through air,
towards some place of trysting. But from the
moment St. David had heard the Angel's warning,
to that of his decease, he continued in the church,

preaching God's holy word to all the people.* On
that Sunday intervening,† after an eloquent and
impressive sermon, which encouraged and exhorted
his audience to persevere in the practice of good
works, he consecrated the body of our Lord in the
Holy Eucharist. Having now experienced the last
pangs of bodily suffering and partaken of Holy Viati-
cum, at the close of a devout office, he calmly said
to his brethren : " On Tuesday, the Kalends of
March, I shall tread the way of my fathers, but you
I commend to the guardianship of the Father Almighty, who will strengthen you to persevere in
those things learned from me." The third day of
the week had dawned, and the crowing of chanticleer
aroused the citizens of Menevia from midnight slum-
ber. Delicious odours impregnated the surrounding
atmosphere, and Angelic choirs filled the air with
ravishing harmonies. With such foretaste of heavenly joys, clerics and monks assembled to chaunt

---

* An old Welsh bard, Rhys ab Rhicceart, in his description of
pleasure, introduces these following comparisons :

> " Like that of saintly David in the choir of Hodnant,
> Or Taliesin at the court of Elphin,
> Or the Round Table feasts at Caerlleon,
> Or Angel joys in paradise."

See, Thomas Stephens' *Literature of the Kymry.* Chap. iv. § ii.
p. 481.

† Giraldus, in his *Life of St. David, Lect.* 10, relates, the saint
foretold on a Sunday, that he would die on the third feria, *i.e.*
the Tuesday following ; and that so it came to pass.

the early Lauds. To the enraptured gaze of St. David, our Lord Jesus appeared, and transported with the ineffable beauty of his presence, our holy bishop poured forth his soul in the exclamation: "Draw me, O Lord, after thee." Thus passed away from life, into the loving embrace of Jesus, this ennobled servant; and multitudes of heavenly denizens led his way to their happy mansions, where not the least illustrious amongst God's elect was crowned with a brilliant diadem of glory.*

He died† accordingly, amid the joyous song of angels, and in the presence of Jesus, who had Himself deigned to visit him on Monday, 1st of March. The Bollandists consider his age to be 97 years, but they, also, give it, as an opinion of many, that he died at the age of 147 years. This last opinion they regard as erroneous, and set down his death as occurring in the year 544. Such mortuary chronology has been followed by many modern writers; but, by others, it has been asserted, that St. David lived to a much later period.‡

---

* See the foregoing account, taken from that vellum MS. Life of our Saint, belonging formerly to the Most Rev. David Routh, and published by Colgan, in his *Acta Sanctorum Hiberniæ*, §§. xxvi. xxvii. p. 429. Giraldus is not so minute in his description, relating to the last days of St. David. He passes over many of the foregoing particulars, as related in the text.

† "Talari indutus tunica," adds Giraldus.

‡ Dr. Lanigan thinks it doubtful, if he were even a bishop, in

On the death of David, the disciple of Dubricius, Ismael, is said to have been consecrated in his stead as bishop of Menevia, by St. Teliaus. Ismael is also declared to have presided over all churches on the right side of Britain.* Now, it is stated, in an old MS., belonging to the Church of Landaff,† that when a synod had been held there in 560, the bishop Oudoceus excommunicated King Mouricus. This sentence was pronounced, for a homicide perpetrated, and for a contract violated by him, even after an oath had been taken in the Bishop's presence, at the altar of St. Peter the Apostle, and of SS. Dubricius and Telians. Such a date would seem to prove, that Teliaus had died some time before 560, when the honours of beatification had been conferred upon him. Now, reason the Bollandists, if St. David did not die, during the reign of King Constantine, A.D. 544, when the 1st of March fell on a Tuesday, he must necessarily have departed A.D. 550, when a similar coincidence took place.‡

---

544. See, *Ecclesiastical History of Ireland.* Vol. i. chap. i. § xii. n. 106, p. 28.

    * See, the Acts of St. Teliaus or Eliud, Bishop of Landaff in Wales, compiled by Father John Bollandus, at the 9th of February. *Acta Sanctorum Februarii. Tomus* ii. *Commentarius Prævius,* § ii. n. 13, p. 305.

    † Published by Henry Spelman.

    ‡ Yet, opposed to this inference, may be objected the testimony of Geoffrey of Monmouth. He says, that on the death of St.

The Bollandists enter upon the following speculative dates, to determine the epoch of St. David's birth, age, and death. Supposing him to have been born towards the close of A.D. 446—thirty years or more having elapsed since St. Patrick had transacted business at Rome, and on his return had spent some time in Britain*—and that David had died in the beginning of A.D. 544; our saint would have completed his ninety-sixth, or died in the ninety-seventh year of his age. They do not think it at all credible, that he lived to the extreme age of 147 years. They suppose it possible, that some transcriber of St. David's Acts, may have fallen into the error of inserting a wrong numeral, in recording those years

---

David, Kincus, otherwise called Kinocus or Cenaucus—who was bishop over "Lampaternensis Ecclesia," in the province of Caretica—obtained the higher dignity of promotion to the Metropolitan see. "Verum is in Legionensi sede successaisse dicendus est, quod etiam innuit Usserius, pag. 528. Kinoco dien mortuo S. Teliaam in Legionensi Sede subrogatum, Menevensi Antistitem ordinasse Ismaëlem, ab aliis dici indicavimus ad S. Teliai Vitam § i. num. 9, quæ annum mortis S. Davidis a nobis assignatum magis confirmant." See, *Acta Sanctorum Martii. Commentarius Prævius.* § ii. n. 15, p. 41.

* In the acts of our saint, he is said to have been born, "post annos xxx.," according to the prophecy. This indefinite way of writing, the Bollandists think, would not necessarily lead us to a conclusion, that St. David had been conceived or born immediately on completion of such a term. Some months, or even a year, nearly expired, might be allowed.

attained at his death. Thus, such a mistake may have occurred. They take Colgan to task for assigning the long term of 147 years for our saint's life, and for instances alleged by him, to prove parallel cases.* Butelinus places the death of St. David, at A.D. 650,† which is thought to have been merely a typographical error; the printer of his work having transposed one cipher for another, so that this learned writer must have intended to write A.D. 560. Edward Maihew maintains, that St. David flourished about the year of our Lord 490.‡

The calculation of Ussher, that St. David had died, A.D. 544, seems to have been founded on false *data*, for it is altogether too early placed.§ He depended on a statement made by Geoffrey of Mon-

---

* In the Bollandist's opinion, what furnished occasion for such an error arose from the statement, that St. Barr, or Fynbarr, had visited St. David, and the monastic habit having been assumed by Constantine, King of Cornwall. These events, however, are supposed to have happened after the death of St. David. The evidences produced by Colgan, regarding our saint's length of years, are nearly altogether taken from Irish sources, and are considered to be very obscure. To refute such testimonies would involve great labour, and it might otherwise be productive of weariness to the reader. See, *Acta Sanctorum Martii. Tomus* 1. *Martii* 1. *Vita S. Davidis. Commentarius Prævius.* § ii. n. 16, p. 41.

† See the Benedictine Menology.

‡ *Ibid.*

§ See, Sir R. C. Hoare's Annotations to the *Itinerary of Wales*, by Giraldus Cambrensis. Vol. ii. p. 13.

mouth, who says, that St. David departed in the
time of King Constantine, son of Cador, who reigned
only three years, from A.D. 542, when King Arthur
fell, to A.D. 545. Into this opinion he was further
led, from the agreement of Giraldus Cambrensis and
other writers in saying, that St. David died on a
Tuesday,* the first day of March. It so happened
these coincident days came together, in the year
544. William of Malmesbury places his death at
A.D. 546,† and also John of Teignmouth.‡ That he
died A.D. 547, has been asserted in the Annals of
Waverly Monastery, and in the Annals of Winton.
But that St. David lived much longer appears, not
only from his own Acts, but from many other old
and trustworthy Records. In the *Chronicum Scotorum*, David of Cill-Muine's death is set down at A.D.
588.§ It appears from our Irish Annals, that St.
Aidan, Bishop of Ferns, died in the year 624.‖ Now,

---

* Not "feria quarta," as Colgan has it, but "feria tertia."

† For this statement, he quotes the Chronicles of Glastonbury
Church.

‡ In *Vita S. Patricii.*

§ It is also under the head, "Kal. iv.," according to an arrange-
ment explained by the learned editor, William M. Hennessy,
M.R.I.A. in his preface. See, pp. xlii. et seq. and pp. 62, 63.
This valuable MS. has been published by the authority of the
Lords Commissioners of her Majesty's Treasury, and under direc-
tion of the Master of the Rolls, in 1866. London, 8vo.

‖ See, O'Donovan's *Annals of the Four Masters.* Vol. i. pp.
246 to 249 and n. (p.) *Ibid.*

in the Acts of David, Aidan is said to have been residing in a Monastery at Ferns, when he sent a message to our saint.   Colgan thinks, that he who had been only a boy, when Ainmire reigned in Ireland,* and afterwards many years a disciple, could not have been Abbot, until after A.D. 580.   He supposes, St. David must have lived subsequently to A.D. 590, and he does not hesitate to allow this bishop may have survived until A.D. 607 or 608. The extreme age, which our saint is said to have attained, is not without parallel in written acts of other holy British and Irish ecclesiastics and recluses.† Extraordinary and well-authenticated instances of longevity are known, even in days long subsequent to the time, when St. David flourished.‡

---

* A.D 564, 565 or 566.   See, O'Donovan's *Annals of the Four Masters.*   Vol. i. pp. 204, 205.

† Colgan cites various particular instances.   See, *Acta Sanctorum Hiberniæ.*   1 *Martii. Vita S. Davidis.*   N. 31, p. 432.

‡ In an article, headed " Longevity and Centenarianism," published in the *Quarterly Review* for January, 1868, No. 247, Vol. cxiv., several extraordinary instances of extreme age are cited, and reference is made to various works treating on this subject. See pp. 179 to 198.   It is there stated, that Iceland, Greenland and Norway have always boasted a large average of very old people, and that the Highlands of Scotland, with " the colder parts of Wales and England, show the same phenomenon in the records of parishes." p. 194, *Ibid.*   Amongst these instances, allusion is made to the old Countess of Desmond, in Ireland, who lived to be 140 years, and according to some accounts to be 150

If we are to credit the account of St. David, as contained in Roth's MS., his days were prolonged to a period far exceeding the ordinary span of life. One hundred and forty-seven years are set down as the term for his existence.* The truth of this account has been denied by some of our most learned

---

or even 163 years. See p. 183, *Ibid.*, and the *Quarterly Review* for March, 1853. No. 184, vol. xcii. pp. 329 to 354. See, also, *Notes and Queries*, 2nd Series. Vol. vii. pp. 313, 365, 431, 432. Old Parr is said to have been born at Alberbury, Salop, in 1483, and to have died in 1635, having thus lived 152 years. Taylor the Water Poet, gives the following description of Parr's dietary and mode of living :—

> "His physic was good butter, which the soil
> Of Salop yields, more sweet than candy oil,
> And garlic he esteemed beyond the rate
> Of Venice treacle or best mithridate.
> He entertained no gout, no ache he felt,
> The air was good and temperate where he dwelt,
> While mavises and sweet-tongued nightingales
> Did chaunt him roundelays and madrigals.
> Thus living within bounds of nature's laws
> Of his long lasting life may be some cause."

It may fairly be conjectured, that a nearly similar plain regimen and strict temperate habits, had a healthy influence on the presumed longevity of St. David. Henry Jenkins of Ellerton is said to have followed the occupation of fisherman to the end of a long life, lasting 169 years. Of this, however, grave doubt is entertained. Peter Garden of Auchterless, Aberdeenshire, is said to have died on the 12th of January, 1775, aged 131 years. See, *Notes and Queries*, 2nd Series. Vol. x. p. 156.

* The Bollandist editor only allows him to have attained eighty-two years.

and competent critics and historians.* Yet, many
ancient writers† agree in this statement, probably
founded on still older accounts, or resting on a
universally prevailing tradition. And, indeed, if we
are to form an estimate of calculation from incidents recorded, it would seem a matter of easy accomplishment, to spread the acts of St. David over
such a lengthened period. When St. Patrick, on
his way to Ireland in 432,‡ foretold St. David's
birth would happen thirty years later, and when this
event as predicted had occurred, a supposition must
be entertained, that the future bishop of Menevia
first saw the light in A.D. 462. St. David was alive

---

* Ussher says he could not be persuaded that St. David lived to
the extraordinary age of 147 years, or until the year 604. "As
to the 147 years, he was right," observes Dr. Lanigan; "but had
he rejected the hypothesis of David having been born in the year
462, he would have found matters easy enough. In fact, that
story of so great an age was patched up to reconcile the supposition of David's birth at that early period with the real circumstance of his having lived until towards the latter end of the sixth
century."—*Ecclesiastical History of Ireland.* Vol. i. chap. ix.
§ ix. n. 147. pp. 474, 475.

† Amongst these may be mentioned, Ricemarc, Giraldus
Cambrensis, John of Teignmouth, John Capgrave, Harpsfeld, with
others. It is said, St. David died, in the one hundred and forty-
sixth year of his age, according to Herman Greuen's additions to
the Martyrology of Usuard.

‡ The Bollandist editor has it many years earlier, or about the
year 414.

after the year 560, is concluded by Dr. Lanigan from the circumstance of his having died during the reign of Maelgwn, Maglocun, Malgon, or Magoclun, by whose order he is said to have been buried in his own church at Menevia. From having been prince of North Wales—and he is said to have lived in the Isle of Anglesey—Maelgwn was raised to the rank of king over all the Britons, about this year 560.* It must have been after advancing to this dignity, that he interfered with regard to St. David's interment. So long as he remained a chieftain or king over North Wales only, at Menevia he had no jurisdiction or power.† It cannot be conjecured, at

* Humphry Lhuyd, as cited by Ussher and Rowland in his *Mona Antiqua*, have this event placed at A.D. 560. Also, in Lewis' *History of Britaine*, p. 204, the year of Maclawn's ascension to the throne is mentioned as the year 552—Vitus being cited as authority—and according to Powel, it was A.D. 580. Ussher himself takes date for his elevation, from Matthew Florilegus at A.D. 581. See *Index Chronologicus. Britannicarum Ecclesiarum Antiquitates*, p. 533. As to 552, the date is thought to be much too early. Lhuyd's computation is one usually followed, and it seems tolerably well established. According to an old book, which treats on the laws of the Ancient Britons, it is said Malgon ruled, not only over all Britain, but even over six adjoining islands or countries lying on the ocean: viz. Ireland, Iceland, Gothland, the Orcades, Norway and Dacia. He is erroneously said by Gildas to have subjected these nations to his sway, after fighting fierce battles. Over these, he is related to have ruled like Draco. See *Ibid*.

† Maglocun is represented by Ussher as Prince of North Wales,

what period of Malgwn's reign—which lasted it is supposed until A.D. 593,*—St. David died; but that his decease took place towards the latter end of it would seem probable, from having had for some years under his tuition St. Aidan or Maidoc, afterwards Bishop of Ferns. This latter saint was only a boy,

---

at the time of David's death. "His hypothesis required this caution. And, lest it might be objected that Maglocun was not sovereign even of North Wales, as early as A.D. 544, he has affixed his accession to that year. (*Ind. Chron.*). He must also have supposed that Maglocun obtained that sovereignty very early in said year, whereas St. David died on the first of March. But how could he explain that prince's issuing orders as to the burial of a person, who lived and died in South Wales? If it be said that he issued them during a certain predatory incursion (see Ussher, p. 528), surely we are not to suppose that incursion took place in the first year of his sovereignty, nor much less prior to the first of March in said year. On the whole, Ussher's calculations on these dates are too much forced; and the simplest method of reconciling all the circumstances is to admit, that Maglocun was king not only of North but likewise of South Wales, &c. at the time of David's death."—Dr. Lanigan's *Ecclesiastical History of Ireland.* Vol. i. chap. ix. § ix. n. 145. pp. 473, 474.

* Several writers place the death of Maelgwn at a somewhat earlier period. Gibson (in his notes on Camden, *col.* 825.) has stated, that he died *about* 586. This is asserted from a *MS.* note by Vaughan on Powel. But Ussher, in his Chronological Index at DXCIII., tells us that Cereticus succeeded Malgon or Maglocun in Britain. This latter was known as Maelgun Gwinedh or *Malgonus Venedotus*, whilst the Cambro-Britons call the former Karedic. See *Britannicarum Ecclesiarum Antiquitates*, p. 534.

during the reign of Ainmire king of Ireland, which began at the earliest, in A.D. 564.* Maidoc afterwards became distinguished before St. David's death. On the other hand, St. David's death will be placed after Maelgwn's reign, lasting until A.D. 593. Ralph of Chester, who is quoted by Ussher, says, that David died in the same year with Pope Gregory the Great. If such were the case, his departure should be assigned to the year 604.† An extravagant calculation of St. David having lived until A.D. 642, founded upon a supposition that he did not take possession of the Menevian see until 577, and that he held it for sixty-five years, has been adopted by some writers. According to this very strange hypothesis, he would have survived, not alone Maelgwn, but likewise his disciple Aidan. It is well known, this latter bishop lived for several years after St. David's death.

---

* See, O'Donovan's *Annals of the Four Masters.* Vol. i. | p. 204, 205. However, O'Flaherty places the commencement of his reign at A.D. 568. See, *Ogygia: seu Rerum Hibernicarum Chronologia.* Pars iii. p. 431.

† Yet such a date cannot agree with his having died during Maelgwn's reign, nor with a notation of Tuesday being the day of his death. Still it indicates a belief, that he did not die until towards the time of Pope Gregory, and very many years after A.D. 544. Other writers have said, that his death happened in the same year, with that of St. Senan. Meanwhile, it may be observed, that St. Senan lived to a later period than A.D. 544.

CHAPTER XI.

St. David died at Menevia on the 1st of March.—His interment.—
Local traditions.—Translation of St. David's relics, in the
Tenth Century.—Canonization by Pope Calixtus II. in 1120.—
Welsh custom of wearing the Leek on St. David's Day.—
Festivals in honour of this holy Archbishop.—Offices and
religious services appointed.

IT is generally allowed, that St. David died in the
monastery he had founded at Menevia.* According
to Archbishop Ussher, his death occurred in 544;
but there is reason to believe he survived this period
for some years.† He died on the Calends of March,
corresponding with the 1st day of that month,‡ and
on a Tuesday.§ The holy disciples of our saint

---

* Geoffrey of Monmouth has such a statement.

† If Tuesday were the day of his death, Dr. Lanigan thinks,
that with a great degree of probability, we may suppose the year
was 589.

‡ Our native Martyrologists, St. Ængus, Marianus Scotus, Maguire, and the Tallagh Martyrology, mention his festival, as occurring on this day. So, also, accord Giraldus Cambrensis, John
of Teignmouth and Capgrave, with the English and Salisbury
Martyrologies. Selden in his *Illustrations* to Drayton's *Poly-
Olbion,* says of St. David, " To him our country calendars give
the first of March, but in the old Martyrologies, I find him not
remembered." See, *Fourth Song.*

§ See, *Ussher's Britannicarum Ecclesiarum Antiquitates. Index
Chronologicus,* A.D. DXLIV. p. 530.

took care to have his remains deposited in the
Church of St. Andrew, within that city, with which
his name and celebrity have since been so much
identified.* Giraldus Cambrensis testifies, that his
body had been interred with great solemnity by his
religious brethren, and that it was preserved with
that veneration, becoming so great a treasure.
Down to the twelfth century, the Lord was pleased
to manifest our saint's glory, by signs and prodigies.
Even in later ages, Giraldus considered it possible,
that accounts of these miracles would be extended,
and added to his own record of our saint's acts.†
St. Kentigern is said to have seen his soul ascending
to Heaven, and borne by Holy Angels. Near the
Church of St. Andrew stood several chapels, which
were formerly resorted to with great devotion. One
of these has been dedicated to St. Nun, who presided over many religious women, and who was considered the mother of St. David. She is honoured

---

* This account is found in Rev. Alban Butler's life of this
saint, and in the copy of St. David's Life, furnished to Colgan, by
the Most Rev. David Routh, Bishop of Ossory.

† Giraldus concludes his account of St. David with the following, *Responsio.* '" Gloriose præsul Christi David, suscipe vota
servorum tuorum, et pro nobis intercede ad Dominum magnum.

Deus, qui ecclesiæ tuæ beatum David pontificem tuum mirabilem
tribuisti doctorem, concede propitius, ut hunc apud te semper
pium habere mereamur intercessorem, per Dominum nostrum
Jesum Christum. Amen." See, *Vita S. Davidis, Lect.* x. *Opera.*
vol. iii. p. 404.

on the 2nd of March. Near this chapel was a beautiful well, often a place of resort for pilgrims. Another chapel was sacred to St. Lily, surnamed Gwas-Dewy, that is, St. David's man; because he was a beloved disciple and companion, during our bishop's retirement. St. Lily was venerated on the 3rd of March. In honour of these several saints, the three first days of March were formerly kept as holy days in South Wales. At present, only St. David's day is observed as a festival, throughout all Wales.* A certain matron, named Elswida, in the time of King Edgar, A.D. 962,† translated the relics of St. David from the vale of Ross to Glastonbury, when all Wales had been so laid waste, that scarcely any one was found therein dwelling. These she procured, through the influence of her kinsman, who was bishop of Menevia. A portion of the Relics of St. Stephen, Protomartyr, had also been removed, at the same time. This religious rite was accompanied with great solemnity, on the part

---

* See, Rev. Alban Butler's *Lives of the Fathers, Martyrs and other Principal Saints*, vol. iii. March 1.

† According to the Bollandist computation, this translation took place A.D. 964, and in the sixth year of King Edgar's reign. Capgrave removes it to a different period. "Hæc autem Translatio Corporis S. David per matronam præfatam facta est usque ad Glastoniam anno post mortem ejus quadringentesimo vicesimo primo."—*Vita S. Patricii.*

of those assisting.* It would seem, that the relics
of St. David had been deposited on the right side of
the altar, within Glastonbury old church.† He is
said to have been canonised by Pope Calistus II.,‡
in 1120. The Bollandists tell us, that either such
was the case, or that this Pontiff must have issued
new privileges to sanction still more an old veneration of the faithful, towards St. David. Soon after
this time, his religious celebrity extended beyond
the limits of these islands, and it was propagated
throughout the whole Christian world.§ The
name of St. David is found recorded in nearly
all our Calendars and Martyrologies, as also in almost every work that treats on the early ecclesias-

---

* We have an account concerning this translation at p. 130 in
the *History of Glastonbury*, written by John of Glastonbury, and
published by Mr. Thomas Hearne, in 1726.

† See, Dodsworth's and Dugdale's *Monasticon Anglicanum*, vol.
i. p. 4. For an interesting account of Glastonbury and its antiquities, the reader is referred to this same work. *Ibid.* pp. 1 to
18.

‡ See, Bale, *cent.* i. The English Martyrology, and Godwin's
work on the Bishops of England, p. 601. This Pope sat from A.D.
1119 to 1124.

§ Nicholas Harpsfeld writes, in his *Historia Ecclesiastica Anglicana, in sex primis seculis*, cap. 26, regarding this saint : " Deum
hujus viri sactitatem orbi commendasse stupendis et admirandis
quibusdam eventibus, quos alii persequuntur." Then are noted
some miraculous occurrences, which are elsewhere related. These
were attributed to the merits of St. David of Wales.

tical History of England, Ireland, Wales or Scotland.*

A singular Welsh custom of wearing the leek has
prevailed throughout the principality from a very
remote time.   Most probably, the leek had been
the favourite article of food used by this holy vege-
tarian, whose austerity of living had been so remarkable.†   By another account, such a custom is

---

* Besides, various works, already cited in the progress of this
Memoir, the reader is referred to the General Catalogue of Saints,
compiled by Ferrarius, Molanus, Canisius, the MS. *Florarium
Sanctorum*, and to many other writers, treating about the saints
of our Church.

† So, at least, the old poet Drayton has it, with some other
interesting metrical allusions to St. David:

    "The Britons, like devout, their messengers direct
    To David, that he would their ancient right protect.
    'Mongst Hatterill's lofty hills, that with the clouds are crown'd,
    The valley Ewias lies immur'd so deep and round,
    As they below that see the mountains rise so high,
    Might think the straggling herds were grazing in the sky:
    Which in it such a shape of solitude doth bear,
    As nature at the first appointed it for pray'r:
    Wherein an aged cell, with moss and ivy grown,
    In which not to this day the sun hath ever shone,
    That reverend British saint in zealous ages past,
    To contemplation liv'd; and did so truly fast,
    As he did only drink what crystal Hodney yields,
    And *fed upon the leeks* he gathered in the fields.
    In memory of whom, in the revolving year
    The Welchman on his day that sacred herb do wear:
    Where, of that holy man as humbly they do crave,
    That in their just defence they might his furth'rance have."
                 Poly-Olbion.   The Fourth Song.

The " valley Ewias," alluded to in the foregoing lines, is situated
in Monmouthshire, and on the borders of Brecknockshire.

said to have derived its origin from that neighbourly aid, practised amongst farmers in South Wales, and locally known as *Cymhorthu*. When a small farmer had slender means, his neighbours, more favoured with the gifts of fortune, appointed a day for all to meet and plough his land, or to render him some other agricultural service. On such occasions, each individual of the company carried with him that portion of leeks necessary to make his pottage.* Others again have asserted, that the practice took its rise from a victory obtained by Cadwallo over the Saxons, on the 1st of March, 640, when, to distinguish themselves, the Welsh wore leeks in their bonnets† Even less rational conjectures have been offered,‡ to account for the early use of this national

---

* Mr. Owen is accredited with the foregoing explanation; although Mr. Rees says, he never heard of such a custom prevailing in South Wales.

† To such event, the great English dramatist is supposed to allude, when he makes the stout-hearted Welsh Captain Fluellen remark to Henry V.; "the Welshmen did good service in a garden where leeks did grow, wearing leeks in their Monmouth caps: which your majesty knows, to this hour, is an honourable page of the service; and I do believe your majesty takes no scorn to wear the leek upon St. Tavy's day. We then find this reply:

"*K. Henry V.*—I wear it for a memorable honour; For I am Welsh, you know, good countryman."

King Henry V. Act iv. Scene vii.

‡ As in the instance of a writer, who says; "Scholars know that the leek πρασον of the Greeks by a corrupt transposition of Pates-on, and Porrum of the Latins, corrupted from Pur-orus,

Cymbric practice.* Of this custom the Cambrians
were proud, from Shakespeare's time, when the brave
Fluellen had. cause and occasion for wearing his
leek, although St. Davy's day had passed, to a much
more recent period, when a modern writer presents us
with the picture of a tall, meagre old Welsh baronet,
stalking down the streets of London, " with a leek
stuck defiantly in his hat, because it is St. David's
day."†

It would seem, that the 16th of August had been
observed as a Feast to commemorate the Translation
of St. David's relics.‡ Again, the 26th of September is mentioned, as having been a similar Festival.§
For these statements, we have the authority of
Greuen.‖

The special veneration paid to St. David in Wales
is evidenced from his day, the 1st of March, having
been long kept as a national Festival, and owing to

---

was an Egyptian Deity, and consequently the Britons, a colony of
Egyptians, were worshippers of *Leeks!*" See, *Gentleman's Magazine.* Vol. lvii. p. 131.

* See, *The Beauties of England and Wales—South Wales.* By
Thomas Rees, F.S.A. Vol. xviii. p. 845.

† See, " London Palaces," by Walter Thornbury, in *Belgravia.*
Vol. iv. p. 464. No. 16. February, 1868.

‡ At this date, we find the following entry : " Translatio Divi
Davidis Archiepiscopi in Wallia."

§ At this particular day, the following account is given : " Translatio sanctissimi Davidis Archiepiscopi in Menevia."

‖ In MSS. Notationibus Carthusiæ Bruxellensis.

the circumstance of that church at Menevia—formerly dedicated to St. Andrew—having been named after St. David. This church and city were likewise placed under his patronage, with metropolitical privileges. Again, the church of Brevy, in the Ceretica district, was especially consecrated to him.

Various offices were prescribed to be celebrated in his honour, not alone in Wales, but even throughout England proper, Ireland and Scotland. Amongst the Provincial Constitutions of England, one is to be found regulating the celebration of St. David's day (March 1st), with a choral service and nine lessons, in the Province of Canterbury.* These lessons are also to be found in an ancient Breviary of Salisbury Church.† In the English Martyrology a eulogy of our saint has been inserted.

In the Scottish *fasti*, St. David's name is found included. The lessons of his office, prescribed to be recited during Matins, are contained in an old Aberdeen Breviary; while Dempster and Camerarius record his name in their country's calendars, at the 1st day of March.

---

* See, Edward Maihew, *In Trophæis Benedictinis Congregationis Anglicanæ*, at the 1st of March.

† Printed in the year 1499. The Bollandists state, "et fere ex capite i. Vitæ desumptæ, quibus in fine Clausula de ejus obitu additur." Hence, it seems just to infer, that the remaining portion of St. David's Life had been distributed in Lessons, which were recited during the octave.

CHAPTER XII.

Miracles attributed to St. David's merits and advocacy after his
death.—Traditional and recorded incidents.—A plague dis-
appears, after St. David's relics had been exposed.

WE are told, that about A.D. 470 the church of
Menevia was at first dedicated by St. Patrick to the
Almighty, and under the invocation of St. Andrew.*
During lapse of time, however, the fame of St.
David spread so much through this part of the
country, and so many miracles were attributed to his
merits, that the cathedral bore his name. An old
chronicler with much judgment declares, that many
of those miracles attributed to him when living deserved to be omitted, lest they might excite doubt
in the minds of his readers. But many undoubtedly
took place after St. David's death, which his intercession procured, and of these four or five deserved

---

* It would appear from Leland, there was a book extant in his
time, *De Dotatione Ecclesiæ S. Davidis*, which he cites. See,
also, Cressy's *Church History of Brittany*. Book xi. chap. xx. p.
245. The studious reader is likewise referred to that learned work,
Tanner's *Notitia Monastica, Pembrokeshire*, ii., St. David's or
Menevia, for interesting historic *memoranda*, illustrating the past
annals of its religious establishments.

to be mentioned, especially as they partly rested on the testimony of credible and worthy eye-witnesses.*

In his description of Cambria—an ancient name for the Welsh Principality—Giraldus Cambrensis records many miracles, attributed to the intercession and merits of this Holy Archbishop of Menevia.† He is not the only writer, however, who has written, regarding St. David's supernatural works.‡

We are told, that a river, which ran by the cemetery of St. David's church, flowed with wine in King Stephen's reign. About the same time, a fountain, known as Pistel-Dewy, or as Latinized Fistula-David, flowed with milk.§ There was a certain portable bell

---

* See, Nicholas Harpsfeld's *Historia Anglicana Ecclesiastica a primis Gentis susceptæ fidei incunabulis ad nostra fere tempora deducta, et in quindecim centurias distributa. Sex Prima Sæcula.* Cap. xxvi. pp. 40, 41. This edition has been edited by Father Richard Gibbon, an English Jesuit.

† See, *Itinerarium Cambriæ.* Cap. i.

‡ See, Harpsfeld. Lib. i. cap. 26.

§ Harpsfeld says, the fountain was so called, " quia per fistulam quamdam et calalem fons in cœmiterium delabitur." Regarding this miracle, related in the text, he remarks : " Quod ab eo proditum est, qui tum vixit resque illius patriæ exploratissimas habuit." Harpsfeld was an ecclesiastic, who died in 1583. He was Dean of Canterbury during the reign of Queen Mary, but under her successor, Queen Elizabeth, he was deprived of this benefice and cast into prison, where he remained until the time of his death. See, an abstract of his life and writings in M. Le Dr. Hoefer's *Nouvelle Biographie Générale,* &c. Tome xxiii. pp. 442, 443.

8

in Cambria, said to have been David's. This bell
had been kept by soldiers, at Raidgnok Castle.
During night, a fire suddenly broke out, which con-
sumed the whole town, except a single wall, where
this bell hung. In a church of St. David,* some
pigeons had built their nests. A certain boy sought
to take away their young, but his hands got fastened
in some crevice, and they could not be removed.
This was regarded as a punishment for his attempted
sacrilege. This boy's parents and friends spent
three whole days and nights, watching, fasting and
praying for his release, before the altar of this same
church. The culprit himself joined in their holy
exercises. At length, as if by a miracle, his hands
were removed from the wall. He lived to relate
this event, to one who had been instrumental in
having it recorded. And the stone was long afterwards shown as a memorial in this church, with the
traces of the boy's fingers formed and graved, as if
in wax. There was a church of St. David at Lan-
thoheni, near the river Hodhen. By others it was
called Nanthodheni.† Here there was a chapel
sacred to St. David, and some holy men passed a
life of strict observance in the wild country near it.
Those who committed any depredation on this
church, were sure to be visited with marked misfor-

---

* Called " Ecclesia Davidis de Lhanuaes."
† " Id est vallem Hodheni," says Harpsfeld.

tunes. Mahel, son to Milo, Earl of Brethenauc, tyrannically and unscrupulously oppressed a Bishop of Menevia and destroyed his church property, in the reign of King Stephen. A little while after, a stone fell down from the top of a turret, and inflicted on him a death-wound. Regarding this as a just visitation of Providence for his rapine, he ordered the church property taken to be restored again to the Bishop. In presence of the latter, he deplored his misfortune, saying that St. David had inflicted a just punishment on him. And with these complaints he expired.*

A certain Welshman, who belonged to the Diocese of Menevia, together with a German, had been captured by the Saracens and bound with an iron chain. Day or night, the Welshman did not cease crying out in his native dialect, "Dewi Wareth," which means "David, help me!" In a short time, this Welshman obtained his liberty, and returned to his own country, where in recognition of his miraculous release, Gervasius,† Bishop of Menevia, received him into his house. As the German was suspected to have connived at this escape, he was exposed to stripes and kept in stricter confinement. Meantime, he recollected, that the Welshman had often used

---

* See, *Harpsfeld's Historia Anglicana*, &c. *Ibid.* p. 41.

† This Bishop is thought, however, by the Bollandists, to have been Gervasius de Castro, Bishop of Bangor, who is said to have enjoyed such dignity from A.D. 1366 to 1370.

the words " Dewi Wareth." The German often
repeated these words, likewise, although he did not
know their meaning.   Suddenly he seemed to have
been brought to his own home, and in a way he
could not understand.   He vainly sought, for some
time, to learn the meaning of those words.   At last
he went to Paris, where he met a Welshman, who
explained them.   The German gave God thanks,
and resolved to set out on a pilgrimage to St. David's
shrine, in Menevia.   Here, he met his former companion, who kissed him with much affection.   They
mutually related those adventures, which might well
be regarded as miraclous.

A great plague having prevailed throughout Anglia, and many persons having fallen victims to it
in various places, it was generally resolved, that
every bishop should immerse the relics of his church
in holy water.   It was hoped, that the use of this
water, by aspersion or drinking, would have procured its cessation ; but the mortality still continued to be very great.   Last of all came the Bishop of
Menevia, bearing the arm of St. David.   When it
had been immersed in the water, this liquid appeared as if covered with some rich unctuous substance, and over it gleamed a golden cross.   The
people flocked in crowds to taste this water, when
the mortality soon disappeared.   Joy and health were
immediately diffused throughout the whole country.*

* See, Capgrave's *Legenda.*

CHAPTER XIII.

Description of St. David's town and Cathedral.—Pilgrimages made to the shrine of our saint.—The list of Rectories, Vicarages, Prebends, Curacies, Churches and Chapels dedicated to him, in Wales and England.

THE situation of modern St. David's or old Menevia is so depressed by surrounding hills, that a traveller approaching from the eastward cannot see any of its buildings, until he actually finds himself entering its principal street.* Notwithstanding the

---

* The old poet Drayton, in his pleasing lines, supplies us with a correct local description, as the city stood in his time.

"As crescent-like the land her breadth here inward bends,
From Milford, which she forth to old Menevia sends;
Since holy David's seat; which of especial grace
Doth lend that nobler name, to this unnobler place.
Of all the holy men whose fame so fresh remains,
To whom the Britons built so many sumptuous fanes,
This saint before the rest their patron still they hold,
Whose birth their ancient bards to Cambria long foretold,
And seated here a see, his bishopric of yore,
Upon the farthest point of this unfruitful shore;
Selected by himself that far from all resort
With contemplation seem'd most fitly to comport;
That, void of all delight, cold, barren, bleak and dry,
No pleasure might allure, nor steal the wand'ring eye:
Where Ramsey with those rocks, in rank that order'd stand
Upon the farthest point of David's ancient land,
Do raise their rugged heads (the seaman's noted marks)
Call'd of their mitred tops the bishop and his clerks;
Into that channel cast, whose raging current wars
Betwixt the British sands and the Hibernian shores:

present very wretched appearance of this city, there are evidences of its former consequence remaining. Traces of old streets may be found, and the foundations of walls, with many other objects of antiquity. St. David's is now only an insignificant village, situated on a small eminence, near a projecting headland, terminating in a pile of rocks. These obtain the denomination of St. David's Head. The whole country around is wild, picturesque, unwooded, and rather thinly inhabited. In a deep hollow, beneath the town, and greatly sheltered from the winds, which occasionally sweep around these rugged shores, the cathedral and its surrounding ecclesiastical buildings are to be seen. The cathedral tower is finely carved in fret-work, and a Gothic ornamental choir contrasts with Saxon pillars and arches in the great aisle. There is a ceiling of Irish oak, which is greatly admired, together with a fine Mosaic pavement.*

Whose grim and horrid face doth pleased heaven neglect,
And bears bleak winter still in his more sad aspect:
Yet Gwyn and Nevern near, two fine and fishful brooks,
Do never stay their course, how stern so e'er he looks;
Which with his shipping once should seem to have commerst,
When Fiscard as her floods doth only grace the first.
To Newport falls the next : then we a while will rest ;
Our next ensuing song to wond'rous things addrest."
                    Poly- Olbion. The Fifth Song.

* A writer of the last century, treating on St. David's Cathedral, says : " This church is far superior to that of Landaffe in its preservation, and has received ample justice from the attention

The Episcopal See of St. David's is situated at the western extremity of Pembrokeshire, sixteen miles distant from the market and county town of Haverfordwest. Consequently, it is placed at the extreme point of South Wales, and even on the most extreme promontory of England, with the exception of the Land's End, which projects more westwardly, about one-third of a degree. The peculiar position of the cathedral hinders it from being at all a prominent object, at any distant point of view. It lies in a deep hollow, immediately below the town of St. David's; and consequently from most directions the body of the church is hardly visible. The great tower alone indicates its existence. Nothing can be more striking than a descent, from the mean streets of this decayed village, upon its magnificent remains of ecclesiastical splendour. Viewed from without, the cathedral displays no great architectural magnificence. Exposed as it is to the blasts of ocean, external ornament would have been worse than useless. Its decoration, therefore, is wisely confined to

---

and expense bestowed on it by its modern proprietors, the whole being in good repair, and the west front having lately been rebuilt in a taste perfectly corresponding with the rest of the structure."—Skrine's *Two Successive Tours throughout the whole of Wales, with several of the adjacent English Counties, so as to form a comprehensive view of the picturesque beauty, the peculiar manners, and the fine remains of antiquity, in that interesting part of the British Island. Tour of South Wales.* Chap. iv.

the interior.　In point of size, this minster is one
of the second order, as compared with other great
English cathedrals, although far surpassing anything
of its kind in Wales.

The ground plan, in complication, perhaps even
surpasses Winchester or St. Alban's.　The profusion
of the chapels and surrounding buildings, including a
college dedicated to St. Mary, the Bishop's palace—
of which it is not too much to say, that it is *unsur-
passed* by any similar residence in Britain—has the
advantage of restoring the picturesque effect, which
might otherwise have been lost, by the absence of
any high-pitched roof.　The whole edifice, however,
is very low.

From the days of Godwin downwards, antiquaries
attribute the earliest portions of the existing fabric
to the time of Bishop Peter de Leiâ, consecrated in
1176.　This prelate is recorded to have rebuilt his
cathedral, after it had been many times destroyed by
Danes and other pirates.

The principal dimensions of St. David's cathedral
church are as follows : Length of nave, 127 feet 4
inches ; whole breadth of nave and aisles, 69 feet 6
inches ; length of transepts (each), 44 feet 6 inches ;
breadth of transepts (each), 27 feet 3 inches ; length
of choir, 53 feet 6 inches ; breadth, 30 feet 3 inches;
total external length, 306 feet ; height of nave, 45
feet 8 inches ; total height of tower, 116 feet.

To conduct the description of the cathedral on one
uniform plan is very difficult; but we shall suppose
the visitor to have entered the church on the west.
Then we may follow out in detail each subordinate
part.

The west front is modern, and it is almost the
worst form of modern-antique. Here we may remark,
that the whole structure combines Romanesque,
Decorated, and Perpendicular architecture. The
external view of nave and aisles calls not for much
remark. These portions of the building form a long,
low, regular structure. The internal features of the
nave are Romanesque, or perhaps more accurately
Transitional. The general effect is very striking,
from the remarkable gorgeousness of architecture ;
in fact, few structures of the same size equal this
cathedral in the richness and elaborateness of execu-
tion, upon this portion of the interior. The flooring
of the nave rises from east to west at a most percep-
tible slope. This peculiarity is probably due to the
builders having followed a natural slope in the ground,
but the practical result is to give the building an
effect of greater apparent length.

The central tower is naturally one of the most
striking features of this cathedral in an external view.
Within, the four grand arches which support the
tower are of very noble proportions, and they are
richer than usually found in large churches. The

transepts without present a tolerably uniform design.
Within they are Transitional Romanesque. The
choir is now the only portion of this building east of
the tower, and retained as part of the church. With
a small exception, it is the only part which retains
its roof. The aisles of the choir, like the chapels
beyond, are nearly ruinous. They are blocked off
from the choir and roofless. The internal view of
the choir is regarded as one of the most attractive
features belonging to the church. There is no lack
of ornament; but the simplicity of composition forms
a decided contrast to the over-complicated design of
the nave. The Lady Chapel, like that of Hereford
Cathedral, stands behind the High Altar.

The body of St. David was interred in this church,
and it seems to have been enclosed within a portable
shrine. It was even the object of Royal Pilgrimage.
We read, that William the Conquerer, Henry II.,
Edward I. and Queen Eleanor made pilgrimages
thereto. The extent of the Bishop's lands, as shown
in 1326, informs us, that the Burgesses of St. David's
were bound to follow the Bishop in time of war, one
day's journey in either direction, with the shrine of
St. David. In the same church, there was also a
shrine, devoted to the remains of St. Caradoc, whose
body is supposed to have been there interred.*

---

* See, *The History and Antiquities of St. David's*, by William
Basil Jones, M.A. In this work, continual reference is made to

In the six counties of North Wales there is not one church that bears St. David's name—as we are told by Rev. Rice Rees.* This very learned provincial antiquary, after very minute investigation, asserts, that the following churches were dedicated—as had been generally assumed—to St. David, in the southern shires. Yet, he does not positively affirm such a statement. On the contrary, he proposes an emendation of the list.† These letters R. V. P. C. affixed to benefices, denote Rectory, Vicarage, Prebend, Curacy.

DIOCESE OF ST. DAVID'S.

PEMBROKESHIRE.

The *Cathedral* (dedicated to SS. David and Andrew) has 5 dependent chapels.‡ Brawdy, V. Whitchurch, V. Prendergast, R. Hubberston, R. Bridell, R. Llanuchllwydog, R., has 1 dependent chapel.§ Llanychaer, R. Llanddewi Felffre, R. and V. Maenor Deifi, R.

Giraldus Cambrensis, to *Anglia Sacra*, Browne Willis, and Men. Sac. &c. &c.

* In an Essay on the Welsh Saints, or the Primitive Christians usually considered to have been the founders of churches in Wales. *Sect.* ii. p. 45.

† *Ibid.*, pp. 52, 53, 54.

‡ These are Gurhyd; Non, (St. Non;) Padrig, (St. Patrick;) Pistyll; and Stinan, (St. Justinian.)

§ This is called Llanllawen.

CARDIGANSHIRE.

Llanddewi Brefi, C., has 4 dependent chapels.*
Blaenporth, P. Bangor, R., has 1 dependent chapel† Henfynyw, C. Llanddewi Aberarth, P. Henllan, chapel to *Bangor*, (St. David.) Blaenpennal, chapel to Llanddewi Brefi, (St. David.)

CARMARTHENSHIRE.

Henllan Amgoed, R., has 1 chapel.‡ Meidrym, V., has 1 chapel.§ Capel Dewi is a chapel to Llanelly (St. Ellyw.) Llanarthneu, P. and V., 1 chapel.|| Abergwilly, or Abergwyli, V., 3 chapels.¶ Bettws, C. Llanycrwys, C. Llandyfeisant, C.

BRECKNOCKSHIRE.

Garthbrengi, P. Trallwng, P. Llywel, V., has 1 chapel.** Llanfaes, V. Maesmynys, R. Llanddewi Abergwesin, is a chapel to Llangammarch— (St. Cammarch.) Llanwrtyd is also a chapel to Llangammarch, (St. Cammarch.) Llanddewi'r Cwm, C.

---

* These are called Bettws Lleicu; Blaenpennal, (St. David;) Gartheli; Gwenfyl, (St. Gwenfyl.)

† Henllan, (St. David.)

‡ Eglwys Fair a Churig.

§ Llanhangel Abercywyn, (St. Michael.)

|| Llanlleian.

¶ Llanfihangel Uwch Gwyli, (St. Michael;) Llanpumsant; and Llanllawddog, (St. Llawddog.)

** Rhydybriew.

Heyop, R. Whitton, R. Llanddewi Ystrad Enni is a chapel to Llanbister, (St. Cynllo.) Cregruna, R., has 1 chapel.* *Glascwm,* V., has 2 *chapels.*† *Colfa* is a chapel to Glascwm, (St. David.) Llanddewi Fach is a chapel to Llywes, (St. Meilig.) *Rhiwlen* is a chapel, to Glascwm, (St. David.)

GLAMORGANSHIRE.

Llanddewi in Gower.

DIOCESE OF LLANDAFF.

GLAMORGANSHIRE.

Bettws and Laleston are both chapels to Newcastle (St. Illtyd).

MONMOUTHSHIRE.

Llanddewi Sgyryd, R. Llanddewi Rhydderch, V. Llanddewi Fach, C. Bettws, a chapel to Newport (St. Gwynllgw.) Trostrey, *alias* Trawsdre, C. Llangyniow, C. Qu. Llangyfyw?

DIOCESE OF HEREFORD.

HEREFORDSHIRE.

Kilpeck, C. (dedicated to St. Mary and St. David.) Dewchurch Magna, V. Little Dewchurch chapel to Lugwardine (S. Peter.)

Thus do we find no less than 40 churches and

---

* Llanbadarn y Garreg, (St. Padarn.)

† Colfa, (St. David;) and Rhiwlen, (St. David.)

13 chapels enumerated in the dioceses already mentioned—in all 53.* Their foundation is popularly ascribed to St. David himself; but probably many, if not nearly all, belong to a much later period, and were only subsequent dedications to the great Welsh patron saint. Four endowments in the foregoing list are of the first class, having a plurality of chapels dependent on them; seven more have one chapel each; and most of these subordinate chapels are dedicated to St. David himself, or to Welsh saints his contemporaries. The chapels dedicated to St. David are subject to churches attributed to the same person, or to other Welsh saints of an older or a contemporary date. Out of the 13 chapelries assigned to St. David, 11 are parochial.† But it may be urged against the antiquity of the beneficed churches, that only 4 out of 40 have endowments of the first foundation. A review of the list, however, compared with a map of the country, and some knowledge of its localities, will show that the majority of these benefices do not stand singly in their situations. They are joined by two, and sometimes by three together;—Thus Whitchurch is contiguous to S. David's, Llanuchllwydog and Llanychaer are adjoining parishes. The same may

---

* See, *Ibid.*, pp. 43, 44, 45. The foregoing list is taken from Ecton's Thesaurus, edited by Browne.

† Ascertained from the population returns for 1831, printed by order of the House of Commons.

be said of Maenor Deifi and Bridell. Henfynyw and
Landdewi Arberarth are contiguous; so are Trallwng
and Llywel; Maesmynys and Llanddewi'r Cwm; as
well as Glascwm and Cregruna. Brawdy and Whitchurch, though not contiguous, are nearer to each
other, than many detached chapelries. The same
may be said of Henllan Amgoed and Llanddewi
Felffre, and also of Llanddewi Brefi and Llanycrwys.
Garthbrengi and Llanfaes are so situated with respect to each other, that it is probable they were
first separated in arrangements made by the followers of Bernard Newmarch, a Norman adventurer,
who took forcible possession of the county of Brecknock, about A.D. 1090. Similar remarks apply to
others in Monmouthshire, and to the three churches
in Herefordshire. Heyop and Whitton belong to a
district, which was one of the first subjected to the
Lords Marchers.

From the disposition of these churches in clus-
ters, it may be supposed, that the parishes of each
cluster formed originally a single endowment, in
support of one church, or perhaps of two churches,
to which the rest served as so many chapels. Light
may be borrowed, on such a subject, from the testimony of Gwynfardd Brycheinwg, a bard who lived
between 1160 and 1230.*

---

* See, a poem, which he wrote in honour of St. David, and
which has been published in *Welsh Archaiology.* Vol. i. p. 270.

All but 5 chapels are in that district, over which St. David was Archbishop of Caerleon or Menevia. The Cathedral of St. David is in the former territory of his maternal grandfather. The neighbourhood of Henfynyw appears to have been the property of St. David's father; while Llanddewi Brefi is situated on that spot, where St. David refuted the Pelagian heresy.*

These churches, however, are not the only ones dedicated to St. David, Patron of Wales, within the British Islands. It may not be possible to present a complete list. A church has lately been erected in his honour at Neath. This is built in a style of Gothic, characteristic of the thirteenth century. It is regarded as being excellently and tastefully designed, with a French treatment of detail and ornament.†

For an account of certain other churches dedicated or specially relating to St. David, the writer feels indebted for the following enumeration, furnished by the Very Rev. Bede Vaughan, Prior at Hereford.

CORNWALL.

At Albernon, there is a church dedicated to St.

---

* See, Rev. Rice Rees' *Essay on the Welsh Saints*. *Sect*. ii. pp. 45 to 56.

† For a more complete architectural description and a woodcut engraving, the reader may consult the *London Illustrated News* of October 3rd, 1868. Vol. lii. No. 1504.

Nonna, mother of St. David. At Davidstow there is a church likewise dedicated to St. David.

DEVONSHIRE.

At Ashprington, there stood a chapel, formerly dedicated to St. David, now to St. Mary.

At Bradstone, there is a church, dedicated to St. Nonna, mother of St. David.

At Exeter, there is a new church, dedicated to St. David, and consecrated September, 1817.

At Thelbridge there is a church also dedicated to St. David.*

The *Catholic* churches and chapels, at present dedicated to our Saint, as given in the *English Catholic Directory*, are as follows :

WALES.

GLAMORGANSHIRE.—At *Cardiff*, there is a church dedicated to St. David. At *Swansea*, there is a church dedicated in like manner to this great saint.

FLINTSHIRE.—At *Mold*, there is a church dedicated to St. David.

The foregoing, we have reason to believe, nearly exhausts the number of churches and chapels which

---

* My respected informant adds, that the above list has been taken from the *Monasticon Diœceseis Exoniensis*, by George Oliver, D.D. The work bears the imprint, Exeter and London, A.D. 1846.

claim David of Wales as their titular saint, in the Welsh principality. In England, so far as we can ascertain, there are no Catholic churches or chapels dedicated to St. David. Those bearing the title of David, in Scotland, appear to have been erected in honour of the Holy King, who ruled over that country in the twelfth century.

CHAPTER XIV.

Historical and Topographical notices of Naas and its vicinity.—
Old Church of St. David at Naas.—The modern Catholic church
dedicated to our Lady and St. David.—Architectural description,
externally and internally.—Statue of St. David therein erected,
with other ornamental accessories.—Conclusion.

IRELAND, so far as we know, possesses but one
church dedicated in honour of St. David—namely,
that of Naas.

This ancient town, from which a parish and
barony afterwards took its name, is situated in the
County of Kildare, and about fifteen Irish miles
south-west from Dublin. It was formerly a place
of great importance, having been the ordinary seat
of the Leinster king, from a very early period.* It
so continued until the tenth century. Around and
within this town, many interesting vestiges of antiquity existed and may even yet be seen.

The principal street of Naas runs in a direction
nearly north and south. The ancient name of this
town was Náſ Laıʒneach, which signifies, "Naas in
Leinster." Tradition says, the first founders commenced the building of this town in Broadfield,
lying south-eastwardly in Naas parish. The spot

* See Archdall's *Monasticon Hibernicum*, p. 335, and *Ordnance
Survey MS. Letters, relating to the County of Kildare Antiquities.*

was even pointed out by the inhabitants, in a field belonging to this townland. Three large stones were laid there, it is said, for erecting the first house. These traditionary memorials are yet visible on this same spot.*

Not far from Naas, and lying on each side of the Dublin road, there is a townland, called Maudlings.† There also a graveyard had been enclosed, owing to a bequest of Lord Naas, in 1782.‡ It is subject to burial fees. A place, said to have been anciently called Fóp Spáṁṁeach, afterwards known as Corpse-lane, near the town, was situated beside a small ford. A great slaughter of Spaniards is reported to have been made at this spot. As heaps of their dead bodies lay in this ford, the place was thus denominated.§ In the vicinity of the town, and at Oldtown Demesne, belonging to the De

---

* See, *Ordnance Survey MS. Letters, relating to the County of Kildare Antiquities.* Vol. i. *Letter by T. O'Conor and dated Naas, November 9th,* 1837, p. 159.

† One of Great Conall's possessions, at the time of suppression, had been " seven acres of arable land, near the Maudelein of Naas, and between that and Miltown Mill." See, Archdall's *Monasticon Hibernicum,* p. 320.

‡ See. *Townland Ordnance Survey Map of the County of Kildare.* Sheet 19. On this also may be seen the denomination Fordspaniagh, in English the " Spanish ford" or "ford of the Spaniards."

§ See, *Ordnance Survey MS. Letters, relating to the County of Kildare Antiquities.* Vol. i. *Letter by T. O'Conor and dated Naas, November 9th,* 1837, p. 164.

Burgh family, there is a well, dedicated to St. Patrick.*

Near Naas town stands a curious old round tower and the modernized Church of Killishee, Killussy or Killossy. Here, the round tower evidently formed part of the original fabric, and in this respect it partly resembles St. Kevin's Kitchen at Glendalough. However, there are distinctive peculiarities yet visible, in both structures.† This place is thought to have been selected for a "foundation" by St. Auxil, nephew of St. Patrick, about the year 448. It is said to have been named after him. His death occurred in 454, as is generally believed; but the Annals of Ulster place it at A.D. 460.‡ A square castle or battlemented tower of great strength stood immediately beside the graveyard. It was inhabited in 1792. A number of caves were contiguous, which circumstance is regarded as a proof of Killussy's great antiquity.§ It is thought that such caves served as granaries

---

* See, *Ibid.*

† Similar erections are to be found at Halling in Kent, and at Little Saxham in Suffolk.

‡ See, Ussher's *Britannicarum Ecclesiarum Antiquitates*, cap. xvii. p. 431, and *Index Chronologicus ad* A.D. CCCCXLVIII. and A.D. CCCCLX. pp. 518, 521.

§ See, Grose's *Antiquities of Ireland*, p. 84. Opposite this page there is a very finished copper-plate engraving, from a drawing taken by Lieutenant Daniel Grose in 1792. It exhibits the existing state of the ruins, which appear to have undergone little

and places for concealment; while those at Killossy were within its ancient monastic enclosure. Although the grave-yard contains no very old monuments at the present date; yet the rank *plateau* soil, with the growth of trees and shrubs, indigenous to such places, indicates sufficiently its use as a cemetery from a most remote period. The approaches leading thereto are roads, which manifest a very considerable degree of antiquity, and they are luxuriantly shaded in summer with fine flowering hawthorn bushes.*

About a mile from Naas, in an easterly direction and on the road-side, there are ancient ivy-covered ruins, surrounded by a cemetery, yet used as a place of interment. This place is now locally called Tipper, a diaconal prebend of Dublin diocese. There is an old cross, with an inscription 1616,† still remaining within the grave-yard. Tipper spring is likewise noted near the old church;‡ and probably

---

alteration at the present date, excepting the old castle which has disappeared. A different engraving of Killossy appears in *Transactions of the Royal Irish Academy*, MDCCLXXXIX. Vol. iii. p. 75.

* The writer acknowledges the courteous reception met with from the present popular and benevolent proprietor—Mr. Moore.

† The letters D. M. W. are inscribed on it, with a sculptured representation of the crucifixion. There, also, is a large font.

‡ See *Townland Ordnance Survey Map of the County of Kildare*, Sheet 19.

the original name was derived from the Irish word " Tobber," which means " a spring" or " well."*

The spacious brick ruins of Jigginstown—formerly called Sigginstown—may be seen on the Limerick road, less than a mile from Naas. This princely mansion had been commenced by the celebrated, unprincipled, ambitious, and unfortunate Earl of Strafford, in the reign of King Charles I. It was never finished, but left partly in its present dismantled state, when he was summoned before the English Parliament, and afterwards beheaded. The groined and vaulted cellars are singularly well and beautifully constructed. Owing to the excellent quality of the brick—said to have been brought from Holland—and the cement used, those cellars are yet in a very perfect condition. Those ruins are well worthy of a visit. Near them, there is a small house-like building, called Castlerag, which dates from the period of Lord Strafford's erection.†

The Leinster kings are supposed to have built their ancient palace or castle on the very remarkable tumulus, popularly known as the North Moat. The

---

* Local traditions state, there are no less than seven springs in the vicinity of Tipper grave-yard.

† See, *Ordnance Survey MS. Letters, relating to the County of Kildare Antiquities.* Vol. i. *Letter by T. O'Conor, and dated Naas, November 9th,* 1837, p. 164.

term "impregnable" was formerly applied to Naas.[*]
Under the North Moat, and directly between it and
St. David's Protestant church, near the main street,
formerly stood the Black Castle. A South Moat is
contra-distinguished, at the present Fair Green, and
on the Kilkenny road.[†] The town of Naas was the
capital of a district, formerly known as Airther-Lifè,
and it became the residence of local chiefs, after its
desertion by the kings of Leinster.[‡] These had
various tributes imposed on them by the monarchs
of Ireland, while they enjoyed, likewise, special
privileges.[§] That the ancient Dun of Naas must
have been identical with the North Moat is manifest
from the Augustinian Friary being called "the
monastery of the Moate."[||] The construction of
their North and South Moat is incorrectly ascribed
by the people to the Danes. The North Moat
measures 23 yards in diameter, the longest way on
top it can be traversed. The South Moat does not

[*] See, Dr. O'Donovan's *Leabhar-na-g Ceart, or Book of Rights*,
pp. 202, 203.

[†] See, *Townland Ordnance Survey Maps of the County of Kildare.* Sheet 19.

[‡] O'Donovan's *Annals of the Four Masters.* Vol. i. nn. (z. a.)
p. 496.

[§] See, Dr. O'Donovan's *Leabhar-na-g Ceart, or Book of Rights*,
pp. 2, 3, 8, 9, 98, 99, 250, 251, 252, 253, 254, 255. Among the
tributes, " the venison of Nas" is particularly mentioned.

[||] *Inquisitions*, xxiii. *Elizabeth.*

present the form of a Dun. However, it is a large
hillock of earth, broken down and encroached upon
in various ways. The Fair Green now occupies its
site. The inhabitants have a tradition, that, before
the present barrack had been erected, an older one
stood on Naas Fair Green.*

The old Lives of St. Patrick state, that the great
Irish Apostle went from Meath to Naas, which was
then the court of the Leinster kings. This is evidently the truth, as appears from the whole tenor of
his history.† Dunlung, the reigning king of Leinster, then lived at Naas. Near this place, about the
year 448,‡ St. Patrick met with Illand and Alild, the
king's sons, and both were purified in the waters of
regeneration. But Foillen, an officer of the royal
household, had conceived a strong prejudice against
the Christian faith, and refused to be converted.
He feigned a profound sleep when the Apostle of
Ireland approached him. The sleep of death, however, came over this unhappy man; and his eyes
never opened afterwards, except to the horrors of

---

* See, *Ordnance Survey MS. Letters relating to the County of
Kildare Antiquities. Letter by T. O'Conor, and dated Naas,
Nov. 9th,* 1837, p. 161.

† See, O'Donovan's *Leabhar-na-g Ceart, or Book of Rights,* n.
[h.] p. 227.

‡ See, Ussher's *Britannicarum Ecclesiarum Antiquitates.* Cap.
xvii. p. 431. And *Index Chronologicus,* A.D. CCCCXLVIII. p.
518. *Ibid.*

perdition in another life. His dreadful fate was long remembered by the inhabitants of this place ; and the worst imprecation they could wish an enemy was conveyed in these words : " May his sleep bo like the sleep of Foillen in the Castle of Naas !"*

It is said, that a religious establishment had been founded at Tulachfobhair,† near Naas town, by St. Fechin of Fore, in the seventh century. It was endowed by the King of Leinster, in consequence of a special favour granted to St. Fechin, as also of that remarkable miracle,‡ which is found related in his

---

* *Life of St. Patrick, Apostle of Ireland, &c. A triple leaf.* Chap. iii. pp. 66, 67.

† In the Life of St. Fechin, as published by Colgan, this place is incorrectly printed Fulach Tobhuir ; but in other instances and in a note annexed to the passage, it is written as given in our text. *Tulach* means " a hill" or " hillock." *Fobhair* signifies either " favour," because of the royal bounty he had received, or it was so called from Fore, in Westmeath, where St. Fechin had his principal establishment, according to Colgan.

‡ To this miracle allusion is made, in the first Life of St. Fechin, published by Colgan, and attributed to the authorship of Augustine Mac Graidin. It is related in some Latin metrical lines. Afterwards, we find a more detailed account, in a Hymn for Lauds, as follows :

"Quemdam Regem extra legem
    Hic adivit et quæsivit
    Ut laxaret obsides.
Quo rogante Deo dante
    Sunt saluti restituti,
    Et expressi sospites.
Rex tunc ivit, atque fuit

Acts.* At this time, the king and his chiefs held a public assembly in his castle at Naas. Within this stronghold, certain captives under sentence of death had been detained; but, at the entreaty of St. Fechin, they were released from captivity, and he predicted that thenceforward, no other prisoners should be kept there in chains.† To commemorate these events, very near the old castle of Naas, and in the market-place of this ancient town, a remark-

---

Ipsa hora, sine mora
Pro contemptu mortuus.
Sed rogatur, imploratur
Hinc Fechinus laude dignus,
Vita nimis arduus;
Ut pro vita sic finita
Optaretur, dignaretur
Adesse propitius.
Tunc vir Dei dixit ei
Surge lætus desit motus,
Qui surrexit citius.
Ac pro dono corde bono
Terras dedit quas possedit
Iste servus Domini."

See, Colgan's *Acta Sanctorum Hiberniæ*, xx. *Januarii.* *Vita S. Fechini,* pp. 132, 133.

* See, Colgan's *Acta Sanctorum Hiberniæ*, xx *Januarii.* *Vita Secunda S. Fechini.* Cap. xxxii. xxxiii. nn. 20, 21, 22, pp. 136, 137, 141, 142.

† Colgan remarks, that this only could be predicated of the old royal castle—which stood on the site of the present moat; but in the more modern castle or prison many prisoners were detained in his time. Indeed, the former jail of Naas—now converted into a town hall—lay nearly between the ancient regal citadel and the cross of St. Fechin, within the market place.

able and large stone monument, known as the
"Cross of St. Fechin," had been afterwards erected.
In the seventeenth century, Colgan says, this venerable object was to be seen in the middle of Naas.
It has long since disappeared; nor is there even any
popular tradition in the place regarding its existence
or removal, at the present day.   The king of Leinster—so the old record states—to manifest his gratitude and atone for his former insensibility, granted
in perpetuity to St. Fechin a tract of land, known as
Tulach Fobhair, with tenants living on it.   A mill
formed part of this grant.*   That place was doubtless situated near or around the principal stream,
which flows through the town of Naas, and towards
which the present "Friary Road" extends.

Congal of Ceann-Maghair, son to Fearghus of
Fanid, made a hosting against the Leinstermen, and
he obtained his demand from them A.D. 705.   This
is thought to have reference to a renewal of the
Borumean tribute.   Perhaps, Congal desired to

---

* This spot is probably identical with the corn mill. at Mill
Brook, near Sunday's Well, as indicated on the *Townland Ordnance
Survey Map of the County of Kildare*.   Sheet 19.   At Sunday's
Well a patron was formerly held.   The site of Eustace's Castle is
also marked, on the right, where the Friary Road enters the town
of Naas.   Colonel Eustace resided here, and took an active part
with the Volunteers in his time.   He was descended from the old
family, founders of St. Eustachius' Priory.   The property is still
in the Eustace family.

wreak his vengeance on the Leinstermen, for the death of his great grandfather, Aedh Mac Ainmirech, whom they had slain in Dun-bolg battle.* On returning from the expedition Congal composed some Irish lines. These are thus translated into English :—

"Bid me farewell, O Liffé! Long enough have I been in thy lap ;
Beautiful the fleece that is [was] on thee ; thou wert safe,
except thy roof, O fort of Nas !
The plain of Liffé was so till now, to-day it is a scorched plain ;
I will come to rescorch it, that it may know a change."†

In the year 861, Muiregan, son of Diarmaid, lord of Nas, and Airther Life, was slain by the Norsemen.‡ These invaders appear to have been particularly rapacious, about this period, in various parts of Ireland. The son of this Muiregan, called Cearbhall, or Carroll O'Murigan,‖ was a valiant warrior. Cearbhall amply avenged his father's death, in a great victory obtained over the foreigners, A.D.

---

* So stated in the *Leabhar Gabhala* of the O'Clerys. It is there said, Congal obtained from them his *oighreir*, or full demand, without any opposition.

† See, Dr. O'Donovan's *Annals of the Four Masters.* Vol. i. pp. 306 to 309. The lines, to which allusion is here made, are quoted likewise by the O'Clerys, in their *Leabhar Gabhala.*

‡ See, O'Donovan's *Annals of the Four Masters.* Vol. i. pp. 496, 497.

‖ This name is probably represented by "Morrin," and many members of this family yet live in the county of Kildare.

897.* Aided by Maelfinia Mac Flannagan, with the men of Breag, Carroll, king at Naas, heading his Leinstermen, drove the Northmen from the fortress of Athcliath, now Dublin. After their hosts were broken and numbers had been slain, many escaped wounded across the sea, although still leaving a great fleet of vessels behind them.† As the entry occurs, under this same year, about the foreigners of Athcliath being besieged on Inismac Neachtain or Nessan,‡ now Ireland's Eye, it is probable they fled thither for refuge, when pursued by the Leinster king. In the year 903, we find this same king Cearbhall engaged as the victorious opponent of Cormac Mac Cuillenan, King and Archbishop of Cashel, at the battle of Bealagh-Mubha, or Ballymoon.§ In the year following, however, A.D. 904,‖ Cearbhall was killed by Hulb, a foreigner.¶ This king is said,

---

* Or 901, according to the *Annals of Ulster*. Here these foreigners are called Gentiles.

† See, O'Donovan's *Annals of the Four Masters*. Vol. i. pp. 556, 557.

‡ See, *Ibid.* and *nn* [d. e.]

§ See, *Ibid.* Vol. ii. pp. 564 to 571, and *nn.* [b. c. d. e. f. g. h. i. k.] The *Annals of Ulster* record this battle at 907 [*al.* 908].

‖ The *Annals of Ulster* have his death at 908 [*al.* 909.] They state, however, "dolore mortuus est."

¶ Such is the statement attributed to Gormlaith, daughter of Flann Sinna, in one of her poems, still extant. She was wife to this Cearbhall, King of Leinster, and a celebrated poetess.

in an old Irish poem, to have been a conservator, ruling vigorously until his death, and owing to his strength, he brought all unpaid tributes to Naas. His death was greatly lamented.* He was the last King of Leinster, holding his residence at Naas.† He was interred, with nine other kings, it is said, at Cill-Corbain, now Kilcorban, in Ely O'Carroll, King's County.‡

On arrival of the Anglo-Norman invaders, Naas appears soon afterwards to have become a thoroughly Norman-Welsh colony.§ A poem on the Conquest

---

* The following is the English translation of an old Irish poem composed in his praise.

"Great grief that Liffé of ships is without Cearbhall, its befitting spouse,
A generous, staid, prolific man, to whom Ireland was obedient.
Sorrowful to me the hills of Almhain and Ailleann without soldiers,
Sorrowful to me is Carman, I do not conceal it, as grass is on its roads.
Not long was his life after Cormac who was dishonoured,
A day and a half, no false rule, and one year, without addition.
Ruler of a noble kingdom, King of Leinster of the troops of heroes;
Alas! that the lofty chief of Almhain has died through a bitter painful way.
Sorrowful for brilliant jewels, to be without the valiant, illustrious lord of Nas.
Although dense hosts have been slain; greater than all their sorrows is this sorrow."

† This is asserted in an Irish Manuscript, preserved in Trinity College Library, Dublin, and classed H I. 17 fol. 97:

"Atá an Nás gan ríg anall, ón ló no concain Ceanball."

"Naas is without a king ever since Cearbhall was slain."

‡ See, O'Donovan's *Annals of the Four Masters.* Vol. ii. ǀ p. 572 to 575, and *nn.* [n. o. p. q.] *ibid.*

§ See, *Proceedings and Papers of the Kilkenny and South-East*

states, that "Le Nas" had been granted by Strong-
bow to Maurice Fitzgerald, holding by knights' service. John, King of England, and Lord of Ireland,
confirmed this grant to the heirs and sons of this
Fitzgerald, known as William Fitzmaurice, who had
been created Baron of Naas. A cantred of land,
which Makelames* held, was that, on which the
present town is now principally situated. The town
was named,† it is said, because the word "Nas,"
or "Naace," in Gaelic, signifies a place, where fairs
or large cattle markets are held. With the lands
and a very extensive jurisdiction, a market to be

---

of Ireland Archæological Society. New Series. Vol. v. Part iii.
October, 1866. n. 60, p. 541.

* This name is Angliciɛed "Mac Callan." See, Brewer's Beauties of Ireland. Vol. ii. p. 55. The old French poem has these
lines:—

    * "Le Nas donat le bon contur
     Al Fitz Geroud od tut le onur;
     Co est la terre de Ofelan
     Ki fud al traitur Mac Kelan."

This may be rendered into the following English translation :—

    "The good count gave the Naas
     To Fitz Gerald all the honour ;
     That is the land of Ofelan,
     Which belonged to the traitor Mac Kelan."

See, Proceedings and Papers of the Kilkenny and South-East of
Ireland Archæological Society. New Series. Vol. v. Part iii.
July, 1866, p. 507.

† It is thus explained in Cormac's Glossary. Dr. O'Donovan
gives illustrations in his edition of the Annals of the Four Masters. Vol. i. n. (z). p. 496.

established at Naas was confirmed, in the terms of the charter. This deed was registered in the 10th year of King Henry IV.'s reign.*

Soon after the settlement of Naas, by the first Welsh-Norman adventurers, it was surrounded by a wall and strongly fortified. Several castles were erected and many houses were built. From its very central position and communications, within the English pale, Naas rose to be a town of considerable importance.† Some ancient peculiarities of the place are on record, and indicate its colonial character. There was a town green, yet surrounded by several humble cottages, where cattle were sold in remote times, as at the present day, on occasion of fairs. Orchards and mills were a feature in the surrounding landscape. A dovecot is mentioned;‡ and as the dove was an emblem of the patron St. David, so was it regarded as characteristic of peace and quiet. Yet, the rest of those comfortable burghers dwelling within and without the walls of Naas, had often been disturbed by turbulent invaders. In 1316, they were plundered for some days by the Scots,

---

* See, *Ibid.* n. 58. p. 539. Also Lewis' *Topographical Dictionary of Ireland.* Vol. ii. pp. 417 to 419. Art. " Naas."

† See, Lewis' *Typographical Dictionary of Ireland.* Vol. ii. p. 417.

‡ See, *Proceedings and Papers of the Kilkenny and South-East of Ireland Archæological Society. New Series.* Vol. v. Part iii. October, 1866. n. 60. p. 541.

conducted there by the Lacies, and commanded by
Edward Bruce, brother to King Robert of Scotland.
The churches and tombs were rifled in search of
treasure, and the town was burned.   In 1419, a Par-
liament was held in this town, by Richard Talbot,
Archbishop of Dublin, and Lord Deputy of Ireland.
This Parliament granted a subsidy of 300 marcs.*

In the twelfth century a Baron of Naas founded
here a Priory of St. John the Baptist.   Under this
saint's invocation it stood, and was occupied by
Canons Regular of the Augustinian order.   It
flourished until 1316, when Naas was sacked by the
Scots under Edward Bruce.   It was restored, however, soon afterwards ; but from all we can learn,
the establishment was a very poor foundation, and
various grants were assigned it, in order to increase
its means.   An hospital attached formed one chief
feature of its charities.†

The present pastor's house has been built on a
part of the old Priory land.‡   A few relics of the
old establishment probably are still traceable.   The
Naas people were once convened by a printed requi-

---

* See, Grose's *Antiquities of Ireland*.   Vol. ii. p. 27.

† For further particulars, the reader is referred to Archdall's
Monasticon Hibernicum, pp. 335, 336, and Lewis' *Topographical
Dictionary of Ireland*.   Vol. ii. pp. 417, 418.

‡ See, *Ordnance Survey MS. Letters, relating to the County of
Kildare Antiquities*.   Vol. i.   *Letter by T. O'Conor, and dated
Naas, November* 9th, 1837, p. 151.

sition, to debate the question of tithes, by the late
Very Rev. Gerald Doyle, P.P. of Naas, at St. John's
Abbey.

Centrally situated in the town was a monastery
for Dominican friars, and erected under the invocation of St. Eustachius. The Fitz-Eustace family
were founders, and its possessions appear to have
been confirmed, A.D. 1355, or 1356. On the 15th
of June, in the 34th year of Henry VIII.'s reign,
Sir Thomas Luttrell, Knight, obtained a grant of
this friary and its possessions. Towards the close
of the last century, a public inn is said to have been
erected on a part of this foundation.* We find the
Dominican Castle and Abbey, with the Abbey field,
marked on the Townland Ordnance Survey Maps of
the County of Kildare. A grave-yard adjoined this
locality.†

In the year 1466, after the English of Meath and
Leinster had invaded Ophaly, and Con O'Conor
Faly had signally defeated them, with the loss of
their renowned leader, John MacThomas ; marauding parties of the Ophaliens were in the practice of
extending their devastations northwards, as far as

---

* See, Archdall's *Monasticon Hibernicum*, p. 336, and Harris'
Ware. Vol. ii. *Antiquities of Ireland*. Chap. xxxviii. p. 276.
This was known as the "Eagle Inn," now corruptly pronounced
by the people "Aigle End." The Dominican establishment has
been revived in the adjoining town of Newbridge.

† See, Sheet 19.

Tara, and southwards to the very walls of Naas.*
The people of Ophaly appear to have met with little
opposition or molestation, during those incursions.

A monastery for Friars Eremites of the Augustinian Order was founded here in the year 1484.†
The ruins of this building were to be seen, near the
foot of that mount, which lay at the farther end of
Naas. At the period of its suppression, the lands
and tenements of this house were of considerable
value.‡ On the 6th of June, in the 26th year of
Queen Elizabeth's reign, Nicholas Aylmer obtained
a lease of this Priory, for a term of fifty years.§ A
considerable portion of its ruins, consisting of a
square belfry tower and a side wall, stood in the
year 1792, when a drawing was taken by Lieutenant
Daniel Grose. The belfry was entered by a Gothic
arch, on either side of which there was a staircase
leading up to three several compartments, lighted by
square loophole windows. Gothic doors and windows, in two different stages, are exhibited in a cop-
per-plate engraving of the side wall.||

---

* See, O'Donovan's *Annals of the Four Masters.* Vol. iv.
pp. 1040 to 1043, and *nn.* [c. d. e.]

† See, Harris' Ware. Vol. ii. *Antiquities of Ireland.* Chap.
xxxviii. p. 282.

‡ They are enumerated by Archdall and King.

§ See Archdall's *Monasticon Hibernicum,* pp. 336 to 338.

|| See Grose's *Antiquities of Ireland.* Vol. ii. pp. 26, 27. A
large and well executed painting from the drawing was made for,
and is now in the possession of, the Parish Priest.

In 1835, its tower, called " Abbey Castle," was entirely demolished. It lay within the graveyard N.W. of Naas, close to the North Moat, so that in 1837, not a vestige of the old Abbey was visible. Abbey field and Abbey bridge, near the spot, are called after the old foundation. It was popularly credited at this time, that a subterraneous passage led from the North Moat to St. David's church.*

Gerald Fitzgerald, the eleventh Earl of Kildare, who was born in 1525, was about ten years of age, at the time when his brother and uncles were executed. He lay ill of the small-pox, at Donore, near Naas; yet, he was carefully concealed and tended by his nurse, who had him conveyed to Lady Mary O'Conor, his sister, in Ophaly.† Lord Thomas Fitzgerald, when he broke into open rebellion in 1534, seized on Naas, threatening to burn it down,‡ and he held possession of it, for a short time. But the Lord-Deputy Skeffington soon afterwards retook it for the king.

As a consequence of intense heat and extreme drought, which prevailed in the summer of 1575, a

---

* See, *Ordnance Survey MS. Letters relating to the County of Kildare Antiquities. Letter by T. O'Conor, and dated, Naas, November 9th*, 1837, pp. 156, 158.

† See, Rawson's *Statistical Survey of the County of Kildare. Introduction*, p. xxxii.

‡ See, Moore's *History of Ireland.* Vol. iii. chap. xlv. p. 260.

loathsome disease and a dreadful malady arose. It raged virulently among both the Irish and English; so that many a castle was left without a guard, many a flock without a shepherd, and many a noble corpse without burial. Naas in Leinster is particularly noticed as having suffered from this dreadful plague.* Not one hour's rain from the 1st of May to the 1st of August fell this year, by day or by night.†

Queen Elizabeth granted a charter to the town of Naas, in 1569. This patent declares, that it shall be a free and an undoubted borough, without reciting or alluding to any previous charter. Still, this royal protection did not save this town from the native Irish raiders. Between 700 and 800 thatched houses were burned on the night after the annual festival, or " patron" day, in 1577, by Rory Oge O'Moore and Cormac O'Conor, at the head of their clansmen, belonging to the territories of Leix and Ophaly. The inhabitants were buried in sleep, after their festivities, and had forgotten to set the usual watch on their town-walls. The Irish carried on poles lighted brands, which, when applied to the low thatched houses, set these dwellings in one sheet of

---

* See, O'Donovan's *Annals of the Four Masters*. Vol. v. pp. 1680, 1681.

† *Ibid.* and *n*. [u]

flames.* The Anglo-Irish chroniclers tell us, that Rory Oge O'Moore sat for some time at the market cross† to enjoy this scene of devastation. However, he departed without taking any life, and sufficiently satisfied with the triumph he had achieved.‡

When Robert, Earl of Essex, landed in Ireland with a large English army April 15th, 1599, he sent a detachment of his soldiers soon afterwards to garrison the town of Naas, and before proceeding on his unsuccessful expedition in a south-westerly direction.

Queen Elizabeth's former charter was again confirmed and extended, in 1609, by King James I. of England. Heretofore, the borough was supposed to have existed only by prescription; and it had been incorporated under the designation of the "Sovereign, Provosts, Burgesses, and Commonalty of Naas."||

A new charter for this town was obtained in 1628, during Charles I.'s reign. However, Naas afterwards continued to be governed under the

---

* See, Brewer's *Beauties of Ireland.* Vol. ii. p. 55, note.

† Doubtless, "St. Fechin's Cross" already mentioned.

‡ See, Haverty's *History of Ireland.* Chap. xxxii. p. 408.

§ See, O'Donovan's *Annals of the Four Masters.* Vol. vi. pp. 2110, 2111.

|| See, Lewis' *Topographical Dictionary of Ireland.* Vol. ii. p. 418.

charters granted by Queen Elizabeth and King
James I. In 1648, the town was garrisoned by
the Earl of Ormonde for King Charles I. He
placed in Naas a new Sovereign, eight burgesses,
and fifty families of despoiled Protestants.*

After experiencing many vicissitudes, in which
its inhabitants suffered severely, Naas was finally
taken for Cromwell, in 1650, by Colonels Hewson
and Reynolds.†

Previously to the Irish Rebellion of 1798, in the
time of the '82 Volunteers, popular tradition has
it, that the Naasians were accustomed annually to
venerate their Patron Saint's day, and in honour of
the occasion to wear " green leeks" in their hats.
It so happened, that a company of Welsh soldiers
marched through the town, on the 1st of March.
On observing the " green leeks" so prominently
displayed by the townsmen, these soldiers became
violently enraged, and were ready to fall upon the
wearers, until told the Naasians were celebrating
that day in honour of their common Patron, St.
David of Wales. This communication altered the
state of feeling, and social enjoyments were the
order of that day and succeeding night. Through
the increase of factious dissensions, however, this

---

* See, Grose's *Antiquities of Ireland.* Vol. ii. p. 27.

† See, Lewis' *Topographical Dictionary of Ireland.* Vol. ii.
p. 418.

custom of wearing the leek was soon afterwards discontinued, and the observance of St. David's day, at least, in that form, fell into disuse.*

On the summit of its ancient moat a watch-house had been constructed for the military, and this small building, yet inhabited, was held as an outpost, in the year 1798. One of the first open acts of insurrection occurred at Naas, during this disastrous period, when a party of United Irishmen, headed by Michael Reynolds, attacked the town, early on the 24th of May. Its garrison, composed of over 200 soldiers belonging to the Armagh Militia and Sir W. W. Wynne's fencible corps, with the local yeomanry, was commanded by Lord Gosford. A very severe action ensued, within the streets of the town. The insurgents finally retreated, with a presumed loss in killed and wounded of about 150 men. Disgraceful military executions and other barbarous excesses followed this event. Few other incidents of historic interest are worthy to be recorded, in the general annals of this ancient borough town.

The site of the old church of St. David at Naas, is in the centre and on the east side of the town. It is popularly agreed, that the present walls of this

* See, *Ordnance Survey MS. Letters relating to the County of Kildare Antiquities.* Vol. i. p. 147, 148. *Letter by T. O'Conor*, and dated *Naas, Nov. 9th*, 1837.

church, are repaired portions of the old parish church
of St. David.*   There were three chantries formerly
within it, viz. that of the Holy Trinity, of St. Mary,
and of St. Catherine. The church of St. David is
surrounded by a cemetery, where Catholic families
still continue to bury their dead. Some remains of
old tombs and armorial bearings, carved in stone,
are found within the grave-yard enclosure. The soil
seems to have accumulated to a considerable height
over the foundations, owing chiefly to interments
continued for centuries past. No very ancient monuments, however, can be found there at present.

The old parish church, now appropriated and re-
modelled for the purposes of Protestant worship,
appears to rest on a part only of its original foundations. On the side walls traces of extension may be
discovered, so as to indicate, that it had probably
been cruciform in design. The foundations of one
lateral transept are visible. It was known as the
Lady Chapel. Another transept probably corres-
responded with it on the opposite side, where a
poorly designed porch now extends.† Internally, as
well as externally, it is an easy matter for the anti-

---

* See, *Ordnance Survey MS. Letters relating to the County of
Kildare Antiquities.* Vol. i. *Letter of T. O'Conor, and dated
Naas, Nov. 9th, 1837, p. 148.*

† On occasion of a late visit, in company with the Very Rev.
Pastor of Naas, the Rev. Mr. De Burgh, Protestant Rector of this

quarian and architect to discover alterations, from a much purer type of building. Hardly in any one instance can the more recent modifications be regarded as improvements. The walls are of extreme thickness. The interior contains some tablet memorials, a rich stained glass window, an organ, &c. ; but it is deformed with a cumbersome gallery, high pews, and other unsightly obstructions and designs.

The present building has evidently undergone many alterations. It is near the site of an old castle which, in a great measure, has been modernized, and at present serves to form a Rectorial residence. It is still known as St. David's castle. The adjoining grounds and accessories are ornamental. Not far removed, an endowed Grammar School is entered through the cemetery gate. Where the steeple once stood, a huge unfinished tower was erected, 88 years since, by an Earl of Mayo. It has within it, on a slab, the following inscription :—*Ruinam inveni, pyramidem reliqui, Mayo.** Some time after the Catholics were deprived of this church, they built another, where the Moat School now is, and which

---

parish, very courteously and intelligently directed attention to many of these peculiarities in construction.

* " I found a ruin" (the old Catholic erection then in ruins), " I left this steeple in its place, Mayo." In the tower, is a bell bearing the following inscription : " *Os meum laudabit Dominum in Ecclesia S. Davidis de Naas.* (" My mouth shall praise the Lord in the church of S. David of Naas.") R. P. W. C. 1674.

served until the present building was erected. The
first stone of this commodious edifice was laid
August 15, 1827. This church is dedicated under
the joint patronage of our Lady and St. David,* and
deserves more than an ordinary notice.

Twenty years after the opening, a steeple, modelled after St. Andrew's, at Ewerby, in Lincolnshire,
set up in the 14th century, was commenced, and was
finished on the last day of the year 1858. It is thus
described by the present Pastor :† " This evening
is one of no ordinary joy in Naas ; for our beautiful

---

* The Priory of Great Connell, within a few miles of Naas, was
dedicated to our Lady and St. David. Canons Regular of St.
Augustine occupied this religious establishment, and the Prior had
a seat in the Upper House. Great Conall was founded by Meyler
Fitz-Henry, Lord Justice of Ireland, in the beginning of the
thirteenth century. See, Harris' Ware. Vol. ii. *Antiquities of
Ireland.* Chap. xxxviii. p. 262. For a fuller account the reader
is referred to Archdall's *Monasticon Hibernicum,* pp. 317 to 321.

† Naas has had but three Parish Priests for upwards of half-a-
century: Father William Fitzgerald, brother to the late Major
Fitzgerald, sometime of Castle-Baggot; and promoted to the
Parish of Carlow by Dr. Arthur Murphy, of Kilcock, Bishop-elect.
This eloquent ecclesiastic, whose memory is in benediction at Naas,
prepared the present Pastor to receive his first communion. He
was succeeded by Father Gerald Doyle, whose letters of appointment are extant, dated from Ballybyrne, county Kildare, where
Dr. Murphy was staying on a visit to a dear sister, Mrs. Germaine,
mother of that estimable priest in whose memory the grateful and
truly Catholic inhabitants of Kingstown are at this moment
erecting a new chapel.

and majestic spire is completed. It was commenced, seven years since, by my venerable predecessor, Father G. Doyle. It is 200 feet high. The style is what is called the *transitional* ; that is, what prevailed between ' the early English' and ' the decorated' periods. The Tower consists of three stages. In the first, there is a very handsome two-light mullioned window, decorated. In the second, there are three long lancet windows. In the third stage, there are four beautiful two-light tracery-windows, the jambs and arches of which are deeply moulded, and have caps and bases. The spire has broaches at its angles, and it too is divided into three stages. In the first, there are two-light-windows, with deeply moulded jambs, caps and bases, and canopied heads, surmounted by handsome stone crosses. In the second and third stages, are single-light windows, with canopied heads and crosses. The spire is surmounted by a gilded iron cross, thirteen feet high and eight feet wide, most elaborately traced. The cross is kept in its position by an iron bar about thirty feet long, which passes through two iron cradles, set into the work, and connected with a weight of nearly one ton, which is suspended over a massive floor. On the cross is a vane, of admirable beauty, in the shape of a cock, remarkable for great richness and lightness combined. The buttresses are very handsome, diminished upon each storey by water-tables, terminating upon the last stage of the tower. The tower has two handsome, newelled stairways, with chiseled soffits. The bell possesses great softness, delicacy, harmony and power of tone. It is a great comfort, and a great honour, to possess so perfect a spire—lofty, light, commanding. The spire is an emblem of ecclesiastical jurisdiction, as the vane is of watchfulness and repentance." The architect was Mr. M'Carthy.

The church itself is divided into nave and aisles by two rows of columns, the nave being 30 feet wide, and the aisles 15 feet, each. The total length from the eastern wall, behind the High Altar, to the western wall of the tower, is 138 feet; and the height of the Nave to the ridge plate 52 feet, a good and beautiful proportion. Forty years after the opening, the interior began to be finished. The following notice will give a fair idea of the accomplishment: "The parish priest, nobly aided by his flock, has been engaged upon a most interesting, and we may truly say wonderful, transformation of the church. Externally the graceful and lofty spire, the elegant landscape gardening, and handsome iron gates had given an unusual character and style to the edifice. But now, under the direction of Mr. Goldie, whose works as an architect are well known, and in the hands of Mr. Meade, the interior fully realises the expectation raised by the exterior, and we think a

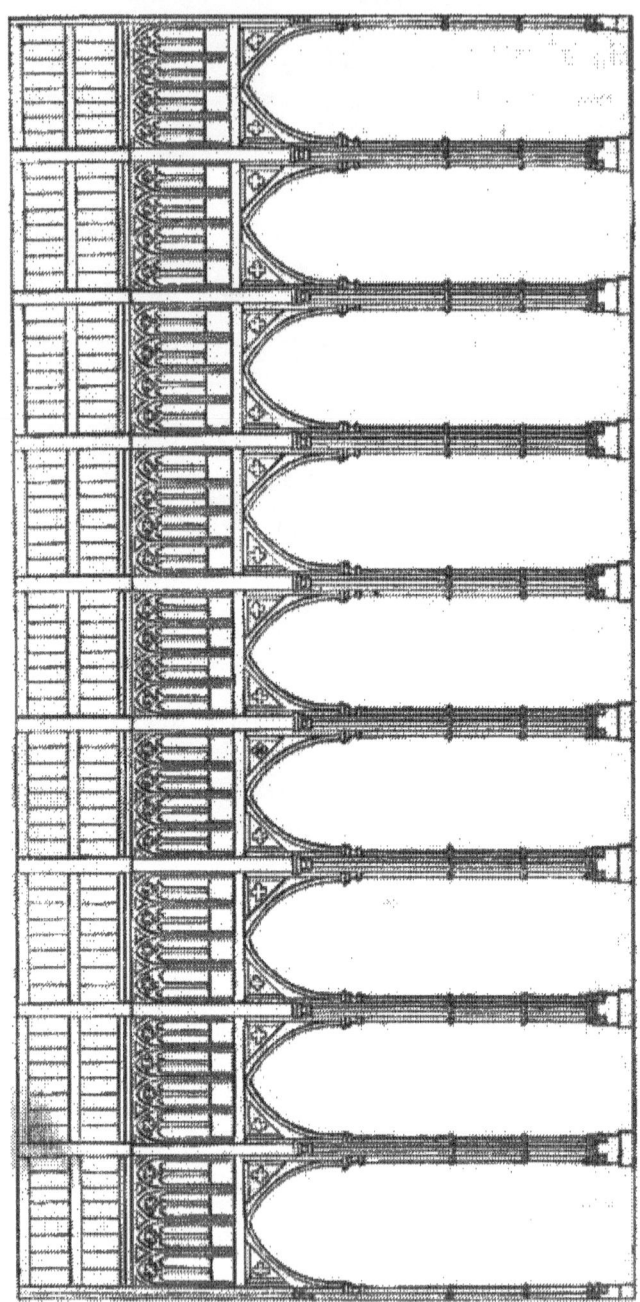

few words of description as to how this has been
effected will not be uninteresting to our readers.
The rude and shapeless baulks of timber, which
formerly were exhibited in all their native bareness,
in the roof and supports, have been converted into
ornamental framework and graceful columns, with
all the accessories of bases, capitals, &c. From
these latter spring pointed arches, forming a beautiful arcade, dividing the nave and aisles, as in the
ancient churches; and over them is a pierced series
of traceried openings, simulating a triforium gallery.
Across the church, and spanning the nave and aisles,
depressed arches are thrown, affording a beautiful
perspective effect, and culminating in the sanctuary,
which has been richly illuminated in gold and colour
by Mr. Mannix, ably aided by Mr. Degnan. The
double gallery supporting the organ and obstructing
the upper tower arch has been swept away, and a
new and commodious chamber for the instrument
erected in convenient proximity to the sanctuary, and
over a tribune for the nuns."

The two central panels of eighteen, composing the
vaulted ceiling of the chancel, are in vellum, having
a cherubim and a seraphim (beautiful portraits of the
artist's children), each bearing a scroll with the
words *Sanctus, Sanctus, Sanctus.* The other span-
dril panels are in azure, powdered with gold stars,
and have purple bands and cream-coloured fillets,

and medallion centres of the cross with rays, and other devices. The groining of the ceiling, mouldings, bosses, &c., are relieved in gold and colour. The canopy of the high altar will next arrest attention, its beautiful proportions being fully developed by judicious treatment. Its general character is a light warm tint of Caen stone and gold, the graceful and elaborate tracery being assisted by a few delicate tints of colour. It is surmounted by the following inscription: "Behold the tabernacle of God with men, and he will dwell with them, and they shall be his people, and God himself with them shall be their God."* The wall behind the altar is a rich crimson, powdered with the I.H.S. and the *Rosa mystica*, the shafts of the columns bearing chevrons on an amber ground. The ceiling under the canopy is pale blue, white, and gold. The altar and tabernacle are enriched with charming devices, and on the super altar are these words: "Thou only art Holy. Thou only art Lord. Thou only art most High." The prevailing colour on the eastern end is sage green, powdered with crosses surrounded by shamrocks, and capped with crowns, the lower portion being draped in a rich olive, having, on a groundwork of beautiful geometric form, a conventional representation of the pelican feeding its young with its own blood; and underneath the cornice, over the Altar of the Sacred

---

* All inscriptions within the sanctuaries are in Latin.

Heart, are the words, "I came to cast fire on the earth, and what will I but that it be enkindled." Above the drapery, and beneath a cresting of great beauty, leading to the statue of our Lady, is written, "Hail, full of grace, the Lord is with thee, blessed art thou amongst women." The lateral altars are a rich specimen of polycromic decoration and gilding, St. Joseph's having as an inscription, "The just shall bud like the lily, and shall flourish for ever before the Lord." In a canopied niche on the epistle side of the high altar, and corresponding with one on the gospel side containing our Blessed Lady's statue, there has been lately placed a most exquisite figure of St. David, in full canonicals. Both of those statues admirably harmonize and contrast in effect, colouring, and proportions. The pose and expression of both figures produce religious impressions in the soul of even the most indifferent spectator. St. David's statue is really charming, while the following words of the mass of the titular of the church run from the niche containing this statue : "Beati David in catholica tuenda fide firmitatem imitemur."* The admirable statue of our Lady of the Immaculate Conception, is a casting in stone composition ; but that of St. David is an original carving, designed by Herr Knabl, professor of sculpture in the University

---

* "May we imitate the firmness of Saint David in the defence of the Catholic Faith."

of Munich. The gates leading to the sanctuaries, and to the Baptistry, as well as the spiral stairway to the pulpit, are fine specimens of wrought ironwork, painted in gold and colour.

There is a Baptistry at the western end of the church, which would well repay a visit. " The Font, which is of Caen stone, is supported on a large pillar or stem, surrounded by eight shafts of green Connemara marble, with richly carved capitals and bases, and eight finely carved Angels. It stands upon a step, the front of which is inlaid with rich encaustic tiles. The bowl of the font is octagonal, having on each face a richly moulded niche, containing the following subjects : ' Pharoah and his host drowned in the Red Sea,' ' Moses bringing water from the rock,' ' The Baptism of our Lord,' ' The Crucifixion of our Lord,' and the four great Doctors of the Church—Pope St. Gregory the Great, St. Ambrose, St. Augustine, and St. Jerome.' The font is surmounted by a finely wrought metal cover, profusely ornamented with shamrock, &c., the whole displaying a highly finished and exquisite piece of workmanship."

A beautiful monument, erected by his parishioners to the memory of their late truly patriotic and popular Pastor, the Very Rev. Gerald Doyle, P.P. of Naas, is in the North Aisle. A recumbent statue of the venerable deceased is there sculptured. It

lies under a canopied niche, with a suitable inscription affixed. This cenotaph is most creditable
to the gratitude and public spirit of his flock.

We should not omit to mention that over the
central chancel-arch is a fine cross, with the inscription from the hymn of Passiontide, "O crux, ave, spes
unica, piis adaüge gratiam reisque dele crimina."*
And as you quit this elegant church, you see, at the
western end, the words a Bishop is directed by the
pontifical rite to say, on retiring from the Altar,
after "Ite Missa est" and the blessing: "In the
beginning was the word, and the word was with God,
and the word was God, and the word was made
flesh, etc." Within and without this sacred edifice,
all portions of its plan and details are admirably
designed and elaborately executed. Adjoining the
Parochial church, the nuns have a beautiful convent
and schools for the education of female children. It
need scarcely be observed, their establishment has
been productive of great blessings for the town of
Naas and its immediate neighbourhood.

It must always constitute a pleasing and truly
Christian state of society to find international kind-
ness and courtesies, with charitable and religious
offices, exchanged between the people of different
countries. Such kindly relationship appears to have

---

* "Hail, O Cross, thou only hope of man; to saints increase
the grace they have; from sinners, purge their guilt away."

prevailed on the part of our Irish ancestors and the
Cambro-Britons, except on rare occasions, when
ambitious, adventurous, and unprincipled leaders
conducted marauding expeditions against those exposed to their predatory incursions. The bad pas-
sions of men, thus mutually excited, led oftentimes
to bloody reprisals. Nor can we doubt, but the
period and contemporaries of St. David witnessed
many of those devastating raids. Yet, it is con-
soling to find, that the holy men of Hibernia and
Cambria maintained an intimacy, strengthened by
bonds of mutual friendship and religious associa-
tions, even from opposite shores. Intercommunica-
tion by sea-voyages brought Menevia within easy
reach of Irish students, many of whom were proud
to acknowledge St. David as their master in sacred
and secular learning. Again, the schools of Ireland
were not less celebrated, about the same time; and
had been resorted to by numbers of Cambro-Britons,
who spent precious years in the acquisition of similar knowledge. We have already seen that several
renowned Irish ecclesiastics are specially named, as
having sought the companionship and guidance of
Holy David. Some of their acts are recorded in
connexion with him, and even serve to illustrate his
biography. Encouraged by his example and emu-
lating his piety, while cultivating their natural mental
faculties, Almighty God was pleased to reserve them

for a career of further usefulness, when returning once more to their native Isle beyond the waves. Hence, in life St. David was honoured and venerated by some of our most distinguished saints, and it is only just, therefore, when he has passed from life to the happiness of immortality, that in our Island, as within his specially privileged Principality, the name of this great and good Bishop should be well remembered and invoked. Through his ministry blessings descended on our forefathers, and so may his protection secure other spiritual favours for those people, who have adopted him as their special patron.

THE END.

APPENDIX I.

DIE I. MARTII.

S. DAVID, CONF. PONT.

Oratio.

Concede nobis, omnipotens Deus, ut beati David, confessoris tui atque Pontificis, pia intercessio nos protegat; et dum ejus solemnia celebramus, in catholica tuenda fide firmitatem imitemur. Per Dom.

LECTIONES II. NOCT.

Ex ejusdem vita per Giraldum Camb. Sac. Ang. Tom. ii. p. 628.

LECTIO I.

David in Ceretica regione illustribus ortus parentibus, sacerdotali gradu ornatus est. Post perfectioris vitæ studio directus, Paulinum sancti Germani discipulum in Vecta insula commorantem adiit: quo magistro cum multum proficisset, ejusdem hortatu vicinis populis prædicare cœpit. Progrediente autem tempore, plura monasteria condidit, in quibus discipuli a populari frequentia remoti, manuum labore, lectione, oratione, et pauperum refectione vitam exigebant.

LECTIO V.

Reviviscente autem hæresi Pelagiana, Synodus in Ceretica regione convocata est: in qua David, cum strenue catholicam fidem propugnasset, omnium consensu, loco sancti Dubritii, qui lubens officio cesserat, Cambriæ Archiepiscopus creatus est. Hanc autem aliʌ Synodus, curante novo Artistite, subsecuta est, in quo prioris decreta omnia confirmata sunt. Porro ex his decretis omnes Cambriæ ecclesiæ modum et regulam, accedente Romani Pontificis auctoritate, susceperunt.

LECTIO VI.

His igitur temporibus Ecclesia Dei maxime floruit. Multis in locis, monasteria sunt constructa, multæ fidelium congregationes in variis ordinibus ad Christi obsequium collectæ: quibus omnibus David speculum erat et exemplar. Neque enim verbo solum, sed exemplo aliis prælucebat, ore efficacissimus prædicator, sed opere major. His autem virtutum meritis, cum multos annos complevisset, primo Kalendarum Martii, mediante sæculo sexto, spiritum Deo reddidit.

LECTIONES III. NOCT. DE I. LOCO.

_____

The Mass of St. David is that of a Confessor and Pontiff, with the following Collect:

"Grant, we beseech thee, O Almighty God, that the loving intercession of blessed David, thy confessor and bishop, may protect us, and that while we celebrate his memory, we may also follow the example of his steadfastness in defending the Catholic faith."—Through, etc.

_____

A Novena of St. David is in hands, and will be ready for his next Feast Day.

APPENDIX II.

The illustrations were drawn on wood, and engraved by Mr. Hanlon, College-green.

The first, opposite the title-page, exhibits improvements, past and future, in the church grounds.

The second, opposite page 159, shows how baulks of timber have been made to present an appearance as truly grand and imposing, as it is light and cheerful, exhibiting the colonnade, arcade, and triforium—*i.e.*, a gallery with triple openings.

The third illustration, opposite page 160, presents the sanctuary, 30 feet wide by 12 (to the altar steps), thus affording the required space for the higher functions.

ERRATA ET CORRIGENDA.

Page 42, line 2.—For "Thermal and warm water fountains," read "Thermal or warm water fountains."

Page 93, line 13.—For "Monday," read "Tuesday."

„ 115, line 18.—For "means," read "meant."